Advance Praise

"*Winners and Losers* is a beautifully written, heartfelt story about a young girl searching for her place in the world among adults she cannot recognize as also lost. I deeply admired the slow build here toward the climax; this felt true to how difficult it is to see reality and to change. Marina Cramer has given us a wise, thoughtful novel."

— Alice Elliott Dark, author of *Fellowship Point, In the Gloaming, Think of England,* and *Naked to the Waist*

"*Winners and Losers* by Marina Cramer introduces us to Lily and Uncle Herman, a grandniece and great-uncle pairing as unlikely as one can imagine. We learn why Lily has come east to live with him as her story unfolds and the roots of loneliness are revealed in each. What drives these characters forward is an emptiness where family should have been. There is a sadness, but also an emergent joy as they navigate through each other's obstacles, past and present, external and internal. Written with intense emotional observation of these character's inner lives and how that plays out in real time, *Winners and Losers* recognizes how much we all need to love those who dare to do the challenging work of loving us through the resistance that insists that life should be a certain way when often it is far, far different."

— Nancy Burke, author of *Death Cleaning and Other Units of Measure* and *Only the Women are Burning*

"In *Winners and Losers*, Marina Antropow Cramer constructs a deeply moving and carefully considered history of family dysfunction. Lily is a smart teenager from an immigrant background whose communication with her father is limited to his occasional cryptic postcards; her mother has been missing for years. This psychologically astute and effective novel probes how we forgive and integrate a broken past into our lives. A thoughtful and memorable family story."

— Anatoly Molotkov, poet and novelist, author of *Future Symptoms, The Catalog of Broken Things, Synonyms for Silence,* and *A Bag Full of Stones* (2025)

"Marina Antropow Cramer's newest novel, *Winners and Losers* is, at its heart, a meditation on family, told through the uneasy lens of characters struggling with their very private family issues, and who illustrate how the lack of family can shape our lives as powerfully as its presence. The novel is filled with the small yet telling mundane details that make a story come alive; the actual theme is never stated but hides in the margins, much like the longing that hides inside Uncle Herman and his grandniece, Lily. It is this sense of unstated emotion that makes these two unusual characters stay with the reader long after the book's conclusion. Uncle Herman and Lily are unique and unforgettable, embodying the theme of family, and also of longing, with their unconventional personas. At the end, the reader will want to give them both a hug—as well as one for the author for creating this very original, engrossing, and deeply felt tale."

> — Martin Golan, author of the novels *My Wife's Last Lover, One Night with Lilith, Where Things are When you Lose Them* (short stories), and *A Note of Consolation for Lucia Joyce* (poetry)

"Marina Antropow Cramer's *Winners and Losers* is as lovely an evocation of yearning, loss, and the ties that bind as any I have read. Isolated Uncle Herman, his grandniece Lily, who arrives at his doorstep in search of her absent father, and Stepan, the home's eccentric tenant form an unconventional but true family. Gradually, they reveal their longstanding wounds to each other and begin to resolve them by honoring what matters most: love. Cramer's gifts are many: her unerring eye for domestic detail, her keen ear for the spoken and unspoken in any conversation, her deep understanding of the past's impact on the present, and her masterful ability to bring every scene to life. The reader will embrace these very real people from the novella's first page, and won't be able to put it down."

> — Roselee Blooston, author of the novel *Trial by Family*, an IPPY Gold Medal Winner, the collection *The Chocolate Jar and Other Stories*, and the memoirs, *Dying in Dubai*, a *Foreword* INDIES Book of the Year, and *Almost: My Life in the Theater*

Winners
and Losers

Winners and Losers

Marina Antropow Cramer

Apprentice House Press
Loyola University Maryland

Copyright © 2025 by Marina Antripow Cramer

All rights reserved. No part of this book may be reproduced or transmitted in any form or by any means, electronic or mechanical, including photocopy, recording, or any information storage and retrieval system, without prior permission from the publisher (except by reviewers who may quote brief passages).

This story is a work of fiction. All the characters appearing in this work are also fictitious. Any resemblance to real persons, living or dead, is purely coincidental.

Library of Congress Control Number: 2025931872

First Edition

Hardcover ISBN: 978-1-62720-545-0
Paperback ISBN: 978-1-62720-546-7
Ebook ISBN: 978-1-62720-547-4

Library of Congress Control Number: 2025931872

Design by Molly Clement
Editorial Development by Jack Barker
Promotion Development by Aminah Murray

Published by Apprentice House Press

Apprentice House Press
Loyola University Maryland

Loyola University Maryland
4501 N. Charles Street, Baltimore, MD 21210
410.617.5265
www.ApprenticeHouse.com
info@ApprenticeHouse.com

For Christina

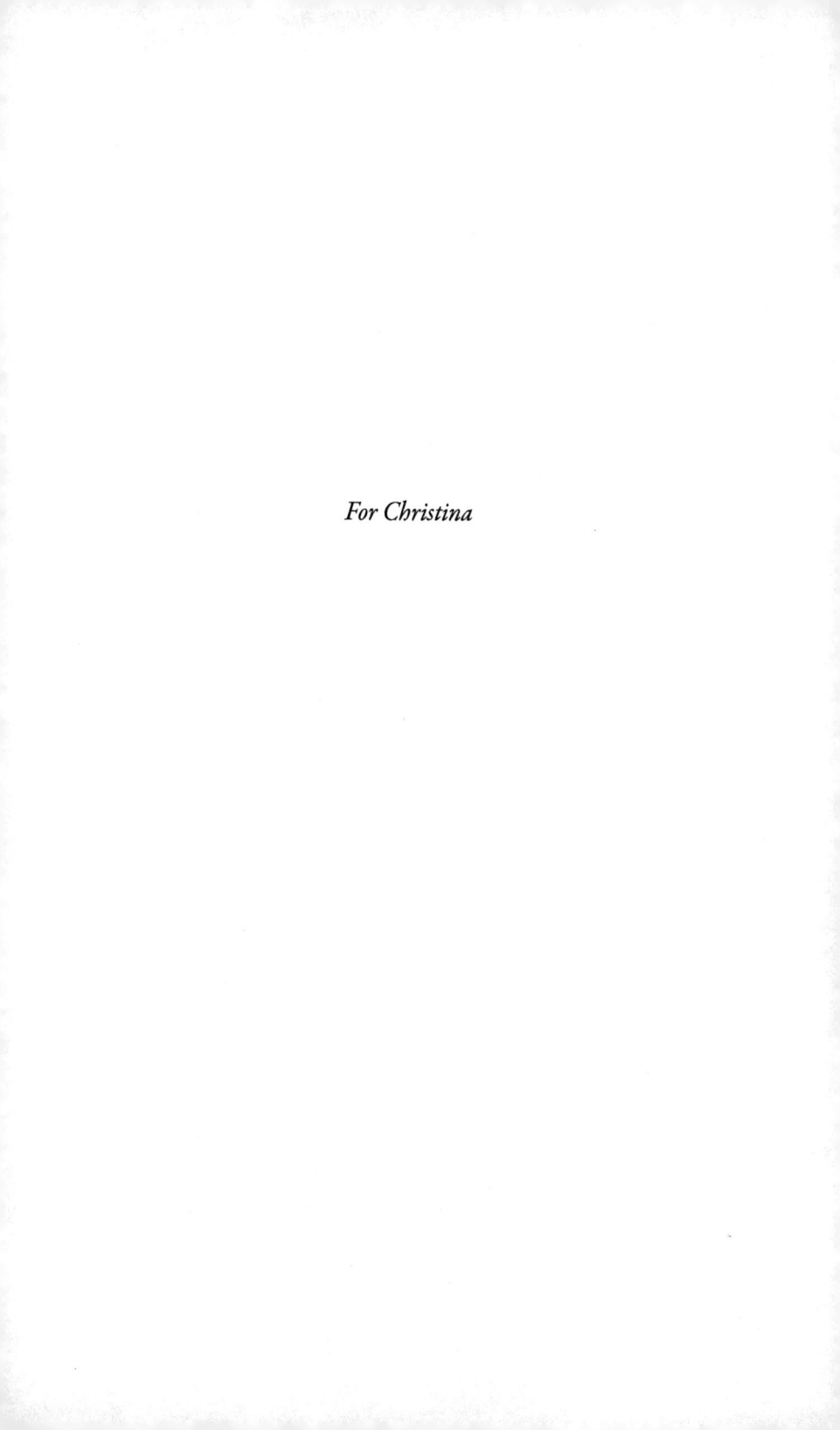

Love, like a carefully loaded ship,
crosses the gulf between the generations.
— Antoine de Saint-Exupéry, "Generation to Generation"

We who knew our fathers
in everything, in nothing.
They perish. They cannot be brought back.
The secret worlds are not regenerated.
—Yevgeny Yevtushenko, "People" translated by
  Robin Milner-Gulland and Peter Levi

And you, will you recall what
you've been thinking behind the fog
of breath that clouds the vision of your eyes?
—Frank L. Niccoletti, "I Am Keeping My Head Above Water"

1.

She turned up on a Wednesday in September, about three in the afternoon. Uncle Herman was just about to take his nap when she stomped up the porch steps in work boots, laces untied, and rang the doorbell like she meant business.

"It's me," she said. "Lily."

"I know who you are." Uncle Herman turned and walked back into the house, leaving the door open for her to follow. In the kitchen, he reheated the last of the morning coffee. "Milk's in the fridge," he said. "Take your shoes off." His chin pointed to a rubber mat near the back door where she saw his safety shoes—their scratched-up steel toe protectors showing through worn uppers—next to a pair of leather slippers clearly too big for his size-six feet. He wore carpet scuffs, brown plaid.

Lily dropped her backpack in the corner, kicked off her boots and slumped into a chair. They studied each other, the old man and the teenage runaway.

He looked small, the cuffs of his flannel shirt wide around bony wrists, the collar gaping at his shrunken neck. His hair stood in gray tufts around large ears but curled, child-like, at the nape.

He saw her cropped hair and tired eyes, noticed the holes in her socks. He saw the way she folded her gangly limbs, one arm pressed between her knees, the other hand wrapped around the hot coffee mug. "D'you eat?" he asked.

"Yesterday," she answered after a minute. She put the mug down, curled her fingers into her palm when she caught his glance at her dirty nails. Then, defiant, she spread the hand flat on the table as if to say, *look all you want*, taking perverse pride in this evidence of whatever ordeal she had just endured.

She devoured the stale bagel, baloney, mustard, in big bites washed down with milk when the coffee ran out. She watched him clean up, his movements sure and unhurried. "You need a haircut," she said.

"You need a shower," he countered. "But call your grandmother first."

Uncle Herman went to find sheets for the spare bedroom. He put a fresh towel and washcloth in the bathroom. Lily, in the living room, rummaged in her backpack while talking on the telephone. When he came to get her, she was curled up on the couch, her head pillowed on one arm, fast asleep with her mouth open, a Little Mermaid toothbrush clenched in her fist.

2

Lily slept the rest of the afternoon; by evening, she had barely stirred. Uncle Herman covered her with a blanket and went to bed. He woke to breakfast smells—cinnamon, buttered toast, coffee. Cinnamon? He pulled on pants and a shirt and stumbled into the kitchen without so much as combing his hair. It was barely five o'clock.

She stood at the stove, stirring oatmeal in a pot. One cabinet—the one he opened only to grab a can of soup or beans—stood open and empty, the worn shelves still damp from scrubbing.

Uncle Herman's house did not suffer from excessive housekeeping. There was just enough furniture, every piece well-made and in good repair and totally without unnecessary ornament—all ornament, in his view, being by definition unnecessary. He swept the bare floors once a week, took a swipe at dust when he noticed it, did laundry every other Saturday.

His kitchen was clean, if only because his lifestyle featured very little actual cooking. He could do eggs in the old cast iron skillet, over easy and perfect every time, but was content with a ham sandwich and soup from a can any time of day. Expanding his culinary skills seemed an unnecessary complication, a waste of time.

"Oh, hey," Lily said. "I got hungry and found this. Hope you don't mind." She gestured at the jars and boxes on the counter.

There were spices with faded labels and grimy lids, some nearly full, others with only a brown or yellow dusting of their former contents clinging to the sides. He read the names: nutmeg, allspice, turmeric, tarragon, celery seed, ginger, cardamom, cayenne, dill seed, oregano, chives. Vanilla, almond, lemon extract, rum flavoring. Tiny, mostly empty vials of food coloring in a little box. Molasses. An opened box of corn starch, the flap closed with brittle masking tape. An unopened bag of chocolate morsels, their edges etched with a dusky bloom. Raisins, stuck together in walnut-sized clumps inside an old pickle jar. Walnuts in the shell inside another.

"What the hell?"

"Oh. Sorry. I was looking for baking powder." She spooned the oatmeal into two porcelain bowls and started to pour coffee into a matching cup.

"Wrong dishes." Uncle Herman stopped her, moved the second cup out of reach and offered his plain mug instead. "Why would I have baking powder?"

"Right," she nodded. "Baking powder's no good without flour. Which you don't have. I checked."

They sat down. He tasted a mouthful, then another. "It's good," he growled. "Where'd you get the cinnamon?"

"In your cabinet. In the back." She pointed her spoon at the counter. "You got all kinds of junk in there. How long's it been there? A hundred years?"

"Who remembers? All's I use is some hot sauce and salt." He made a crater in his oatmeal and filled it with milk. Fine rivulets spread to the edges of the bowl before disappearing into the aromatic mass. Lily watched him, watched the spoon in his knobby fingers stir the milk around in a motion so habitual it seemed almost like a ritual.

They ate.

It wasn't until Lily stacked the empty bowls in the sink that she remembered Uncle Herman's words. "Why wrong, the dishes? I like them." She held up her coffee cup. The porcelain had a sheen like thick cream, with a scattering of hand-painted violets and pale green leaves.

"Not mine," he replied. He motioned at the shelf that held the rest of the set. "That's Stepan's stuff."

"Who's Stepan?" she paused. "Oh, I get it. The guy with the big feet." She glanced at the leather slippers by the door.

"Yeah. My tenant. That's his food in the freezer, leave it alone." He clamped his mouth closed as if exhausted by all the talking, shooed her aside to wash the dishes himself.

"Where is he?"

"Away. He sells books. Travels around."

"Oh."

Lily turned her attention to the contents of the emptied cabinet. She sorted things into two groupings, shaking or sniffing what was inside before deciding where it should go. She finished just as Uncle Herman put the dried bowls away. "Okay, look," she said. "You got winners and losers here. These are still good. They're not real strong or fresh, but they're okay to use." She pointed at some spice jars, cornstarch, molasses. "These—" she pointed at the herbs and empty containers, "these are like, a waste." She picked up a big jar of chives, their once-green color aged to a nearly transparent gray. "They'll taste like dry grass. Not even."

He waved a dismissive hand. "Throw them out. Don't need 'em."

"Cool. Where'd it all come from anyway? Why'd you keep it?" She gathered up the losers and dumped them in the trash.

"Dunno," he mumbled, starting for the door to his room. "Nora, maybe. Too many questions."

He didn't shuffle, but his steps had a grave, deliberate quality as if he needed to know exactly where to place his feet to guide them to their destination. Lily watched him retreat, his back straight,

5

head down.

"Uncle Herman?" She took a deep breath. "Take me shopping and I'll make scones tomorrow. I can try soaking the raisins."

"Deal," he answered without turning around. "Need birdseed, anyway."

"Uncle Herman?" Something in her voice, a high-pitched note with an underlying tremor of uncertainty, made him half-turn and study her from under unruly eyebrows, his head cocked to one side like a bird eyeing a worm. "Don't you want to know why I came?"

"You'll tell me."

He went into the bathroom and closed the door.

3

In the meat department, Uncle Herman picked up some hot dogs on sale. "I can make chicken if you want," Lily offered.

He shrugged, let her choose, and moved on to dairy. "How long you staying? Get the sale eggs, and margarine."

She put the items in the cart. "Butter tastes better," she said, then added, "I don't know yet. Grams said it was okay if you're good with it. Get this—she had the California cops out looking for me like I was hustling my ass on the street or something."

He stopped the cart and stared at her. "What'd you expect? You're what, fourteen?"

"Yeah, but I'm not a baby. So, butter? Makes everything taste good."

"At three times the price. Get the half."

"It's cheaper by the pound and stays fresh in the freezer. You think Stepan would mind? If we use the freezer, I mean."

"My house. My fridge."

For a moment, Uncle Herman considered telling her about the arrangement. He thought of the deed, changed to Stepan's name in 1990, before Lily was born. According to the legal paperwork, he and Stepan continued to split the bills, and Uncle Herman had an uncontested right of occupancy for the rest of his life. Not the time or place, he decided now. Too much talking and right now, beside the point. "Take the damn butter," he said. "I don't have all day."

You don't? Lily almost said but stopped herself. This old man was nothing like his sister, her placid grandmother. She couldn't read him, didn't know how deep the crankiness went, how far she could count on family ties. She walked ahead of the cart and turned into the baking aisle.

When he caught up, she was waiting with a sack of flour, baking powder, and baking soda.

"Both?" He frowned. "You said powder."

"You need both for like, muffins."

"Muffins," he growled. He added something else, something that sounded like, "pain in the ass women." Lily couldn't be sure, so when he replaced the green-striped package of organic sugar with the no-frills store brand, she thought it best to let it go.

At the end of the aisle, in international food, she found rice and soy sauce. "For the chicken," she answered his raised eyebrows. "I'm done. Oh, wait." She ran off, came back with garlic and two lemons. "Okay now. Thanks." He didn't return her smile. On the way out, he tossed in five cans of the cheapest tuna, four each of baked beans and corned beef hash. Then, as if remembering he had company, he added two more of each.

The checkout line moved slowly. They inched along in silence, not looking at each other, until she said, "You forgot birdseed."

"Not here. Feed store." The words fell off his tongue as if cut with a knife. She had no idea what they meant, what a feed store was. Must be some farm thing, she guessed, but knew enough to shut her mouth.

He paid and handed her the bags to carry. In the car, she kept her head turned to the window. The New York landscape rolled out fields, a few cows, a herd of goats, signs for eggs and hay and manure for sale. Trees, trees, trees.

The Agway parking lot was lined on one side with stacks of fertilizer in heavy sacks, piles of mulch and wood chips by the truckload. Pots of fall flowers rose in neat rows near the store's open door, arranged on a weathered wood display that reminded Lily of school bleachers back home. Uncle Herman had turned off the ignition and had one foot on the ground when she asked, "Is there a bus from here to West Point?"

4

Uncle Herman wasn't a cautious man, except with his heart.

Both his parents had been orphaned by the first wave of the 1890 Russian flu epidemic that swept the globe with a swift fury never before experienced by humanity, afflicting ordinary folk and the Imperial family with equal ferocity. Carried by travelers on Europe's proud new railroads, it engulfed the continent and found its way to New York on board transatlantic vessels, taking victims indiscriminately among passengers and crew.

Whether it was the witness of so much death and suffering or their own determination to build themselves the family they had been denied, it's hard to say. His parents married and filled their home with children, mixing their nine with several they adopted between bouts of fertility. The eldest helped raise the ones who came later; somehow, there were always enough beds, and no one went hungry. It was chaotic and wonderful.

Herman was next to the last. Within a few years of his birth, people around him started to die. In 1918, when Herman was two, the eldest fell at Ypres as the war in Europe was winding down. Mustard gas poisoning took the next one, who was only just old enough to serve. A third survived the fighting but succumbed to the Spanish flu on the troop ship bound for New York. He was buried at sea according to regulations, and to forestall the possibility of contagion.

It was as if those deaths opened the door to disaster. Random misfortune picked off those brothers and sisters, some of whom he was just getting to know, in ones and twos. A boating accident on Lake Michigan, a winter train wreck in Austria. A house fire claimed Herman's elderly parents, several visiting grandchildren, and even the beloved arthritic family dog.

Others perished in less dramatic but equally tragic ways: measles, scarlet fever, emphysema, cardiac arrest, kidney failure, cancer.

Herman grew reckless in the face of so much loss, such relentless grief. He smoked heavily, drove like a maniac, drank too much. But he learned to guard his heart. Women puzzled him. He liked their grace, their competence and resiliency, but was baffled by their need for conversation. One by one, they walked away from his taciturn ways, his refusal to risk anything at all for love. Even Nora.

5

His house stood at the edge of the workers' village built in the 1930s to accommodate the Hudson Valley candy factory's employees and their families. The factory had taken him on right out of high school as a machinist's apprentice. When the war came, he served willingly enough, with ordinary bravery undistinguished by any acts of heroism.

After the bombing of Nagasaki ended the war, he returned to the factory, shared the three-bedroom house with two other vets rent-free for eighteen months as a token of the nation's gratitude and an inducement to stay put and keep the confections flowing through smoothly maintained machinery. It was a good job. "Everybody needs candy," he liked to say. "Even bears steal honey from the bees."

He stayed put, with a succession of housemates who eventually married or moved on to postwar upwardly mobile careers. He earned respect at work in spite of his prickly personality. Everyone knew you couldn't ask about his family or talk to him about the baseball game. He had no interest in playing cards, joining the bowling league, or getting a few beers after work. But he knew the metallic soul of every piece of candy-making equipment, understood each screw, belt, valve, and piston better than anyone, before or since.

When the main conveyor belt at the candy factory broke down, threatening the cancellation of the biggest contract in the company's history, the shop steward said, "Get Uncle Herman."

The machinery got fixed in record time, and the name stuck, with no one but Herman fully aware of its irony.

In the restless 60s, when young families began to manifest a marked desire to make their own living arrangements, he bought the house from the factory at a fraction of its market value. It had a new roof, a big enough yard, trees. Uncle Herman added insulation and installed a row of bird feeders under the white pine near the southwest corner of the property. The pine provided afternoon shade and year-round cover—scads of finches, juncos, grosbeaks, and woodpeckers entertained him daily with their songs and amused him with their squabbling. That the feeders could only be observed from the bathroom window did not amount to an inconvenience. His long-time tenant Stepan worked during the day and sometimes traveled, and no one watches birds after dark.

By 2000, the tribe was pared down to one sister, Stella, who lived on the west coast; her son Mark, a career Army man whom Herman couldn't say he knew, and Mark's daughter Lily, a grandniece Uncle Herman watched grow into adolescence through a stream of annual photographs.

He and Stella exchanged visits in the early years, but found, as they aged, they had little in common—or not enough to justify a life change that would bring them closer together.

"I like the sun," Stella said the one time they discussed the possibility of her moving east. "And the beach. My friends are widows, like me; we keep each other entertained. And, I have Lily to raise, don't I. This is her home." That Herman might move west, or anywhere, was so clearly out of the question it was never even brought up.

Reluctant to leave the only job he'd ever had, he worked well past ordinary retirement age. He grew used to his solitude, filled his evening hours with books from the library. By day, he was content to walk in the woods, watch the birds at his feeders, keep the house in good repair, and tinker with his car just enough to keep it going.

Stepan was the ideal housemate. His travels kept him away several days a week. He was quiet, cleaned up after himself, didn't smoke, paid his rent on time, and never brought women home.

6

The first postcard, addressed to Stella and, in parentheses under her name, *the child*, arrived on Lily's third birthday. The picture side showed a snowman, a frayed black scarf, shot through with holes, loosely tied around its neck. A floppy hat obscured all of its face except for a grim pebble mouth, the stones embedded in a ragged line like decaying teeth.

The message side had a large hand-drawn capital letter A, its diminutive cursive version curled beside the sturdy base. Next to the graphic, in the same black ink, were the words:

> A, first letter of the alphabet. Its Greek correspondent is named alpha. It is a usual symbol for a low central vowel as in father. In musical notation it is the symbol of a note on the scale.
>
> Yours Truly

There was no signature, no name except in the military APO return address. Along the bottom edge, in clear but tiny script, was the attribution—*The Columbia Encyclopedia*, Third Edition, Columbia U Press, 1963, William Bridgwater and Seymour Kurtz (eds.)

Stella's impulse was to throw the damn thing away. What kind of greeting was this to send a small child? A toddler who hadn't heard a word from her father since he'd boarded a cross-country bus for West Point, only a few weeks after the disappearance of his wayward young wife. And now this?

"You can hold her," Stella remembered telling her son. "She won't break."

Mark had picked the baby up and held her out at arm's length, his bent elbows stiff as a department store clothes mannequin's. Stella watched his ears redden the way they did whenever he gave in to emotion—joy, surprise, anger, guilt, fear. She didn't know which combination he was feeling now.

"Take her. Take her, Mom." He handed Stella the infant, sat down and passed a hand over his mouth and chin, his fingers trembling. "I mean, you take her. I mean, diapers, bottles, baby food, clothes…" His voice trailed off as if even talking about caring for a child was too horrific to contemplate. "What if she gets sick?" He looked so distraught that Stella almost pitied him. "It's either you or a foster home."

"And her mother?"

"She's strung out, grooving with her hippie friends. She'll be lucky to make it to seventeen." Mark confirmed what they both knew. "Help me, Mom. What do I know about babies?"

"What do you know about anything?" The words spilled out of Stella's mouth before she could bite them back. It was too late; she might as well say it all now. "You're twenty-nine and too busy chasing high school girls to figure out what to do with your life." She looked away. "It takes money to raise a child, Mark. You know how I've struggled since your father died."

"Well, I won't be peddling any more life insurance, that's for sure. I've had enough of that disaster. I'm enlisting in the Army. I can learn something, and the pay's steady. I won't forget you, or—" he nodded at the baby sleeping in her thrift-store crib. "Her."

"Lily," Stella said. "Her name is Lily."

Stella had to admit he'd been good as his word this time. The money came once a month, with a brief note—doing okay, take care of yourself, going overseas—but there had been nothing for Lily. Until now.

"And look at it," she said to her neighbor over their mid-morning coffee. "Who sends something this gruesome to a child?"

"Does she even know what snow is? Living here in California?" Margrit replied.

Stella sighed. Margrit was kind, but her words were seldom helpful.

Before Stella could toss it in the trash, Lily picked the card up from the kitchen table. Stella couldn't guess what went through her mind, couldn't read the wicked little smile that played around her granddaughter's lips. Then Lily laughed, with total full-throated body-and-soul delight. She mirrored the snowman's unsmiling expression, stretching her soft baby mouth into a straight line between spells of hilarity. She turned the card over and traced the big A with the tip of her finger, her face lit up with wonder and curiosity.

"It's for you," Stella told her with a sigh. "From your father." She almost said *Daddy*, but the word seemed wrong, too casual, out of sync with the somber formality of the card. "He must think you've never seen the alphabet before," she added under her breath.

Ten days later there was another card—a carousel of horses, tigers, elephants, giraffes—all with fierce painted eyes, their polished backs worn smooth by untold numbers of happy riders. On the reverse, this:

> Animal. Most animals have specialized means of locomotion, possess nervous systems and sense organs, and are

adapted for securing, ingesting, and digesting food. The scientific study of animals is called ZOOLOGY.

Yours Truly

The words were adorned with ink sketches of various beasts—a mouse, a squirrel, an ox, a pelican—the drawings crowded into the scant space around the text. They were surprisingly good, with just enough detail for easy identification. There was no greeting, signature, or personal message.

"Why doesn't he send her a picture book, for children?" Margrit said. "That would be easier, and better."

"Easier," Stella sniffed. "Mark has never done what's easier. It's not his way. Imagine, though," she added. "I'm his mother and I never knew he could draw like that."

She gave Lily the card, along with a square cookie tin that still smelled of sugar and vanilla. "For your cards," she said, because Mark was also methodical. There would be more, of that she was sure.

The third card was a painting, a village wedding. Men in cloth caps and breeches, kerchiefed women in layered skirts. Casks of ale, a fiddler. Children everywhere. The revelers in motion, intent on celebration, while evening settled among the trees.

Stella studied this scene for a long time. She kept the card for a day or two on her nightstand before giving it to Lily. Among the encroaching shadows of gray and brown, she liked the billow of a white sleeve, the flash of a yellow vest. The enticing triangle of a scarlet petticoat.

On the back, in black ink, Mark had written:

> Annual. Plant that germinates, blossoms, and dies within one growing season. Annuals propagate themselves by seed only. Hardy annuals are usually sown where they are

expected to bloom.

Yours Truly

Around the edges, he had sketched a pepper, a cucumber, an ear of corn, a sunflower, zinnia, petunias. Along the bottom edge, the same scholarly attribution. No greeting. No signature.

"You're a strange one, Mark," Stella said before she turned out the light. No point wondering what connection he implied between a country wedding and a gardening lesson. Maybe none; maybe it was the only card he could find at the time.

Lily held the card with both hands. She moved it back and forth, squinting as if looking for a hidden message or trying to bring the dancing figures to life. She looked up, her round face serious. "Father? For Lily?"

"Father. For Lily," Stella echoed, suppressing the faint stirring of envy that made her eyes prickle with tears. Even without addressing his daughter, with no personal message or signature, the correspondence seemed more intimate than the dutiful letters he wrote to her, his mother—letters that held scant details and little feeling. *Easy to be playful*, she thought, *when you are miles away, with no worry about how your child is being raised.* Stella had to admit, though, that while she took on the unexpected parenting role with genuine love and serious purpose, playfulness was not in her nature.

The child ran off and came back with the cookie tin. She plopped herself down on the couch next to her grandmother, retrieved all three cards and thrust them at Stella. "Read," she commanded.

7

Stepan kept his hair short on the sides, long in the front, so it could wave forward over his forehead the way it had when he was young. The back was trimmed collar-length. He'd been coloring his hair since the first gray glinted in the mirror and sent him, with unexpected urgency, to the drug store for dye, making him miss that day's first two appointments. It couldn't be helped, he reasoned. Booksellers tended to stay in their shops and take care of business. He could see them another day.

There was the thinning spot, he knew, on the crown. It troubled him. He started to look into weaves and other measures but decided it needed to get worse before he could justify the expense. Besides, he was over six feet, with a ready laugh and a quick wit, good posture and no paunch. He liked his women no higher than his shoulder; the few exceptions to this rule had been decidedly regrettable. Tall women tended to a wearisome self-confidence he preferred to do without. There was no reason for anyone but his barber to see the top of his head. Except maybe in bed, but by then it hardly mattered.

Lately, he'd been thinking of trying a silver streak, just there, where the hair came down and brushed his eyebrow. He thought it might add dignity and dash to his appearance; that it would draw women to him, he had no doubt. After receiving a surprisingly generous commission check, he treated himself to a city adventure that included a stop at a swank salon—the kind of place where they flash your picture on a screen and let you try on different styles to see if you like it. He liked it.

"You said you're from Hungary, right?" Lily put the book down, still open, in her lap. She was reading her way through Uncle Herman's 1970s *Encyclopedia Britannica*.

Stepan looked up from his order pad. "Why do you ask?"

It irked him that every other sales rep he knew had a company-issue laptop. Only his employer—a struggling consortium of small independent presses specializing in arcane scholarly tomes, literary translations, experimental fiction, and, naturally, poetry—had yet to take the leap into the digital age. They had established a fledgling web presence for libraries and the academic market, but trade orders still had to be turned in the time-honored way, on paper.

"The way you spell your name. It should be Stefan, with an f, if you're from Hungary."

"Not necessarily." He looked at her over his reading glasses. She would be tall, that one, if she didn't stop growing soon. "Your name, for instance: Lily. You could spell it half a dozen different ways, none of them wrong."

"Huh." Lily went into the kitchen and came back with a glass of lemonade.

Stepan capped his pen and slipped it into his shirt pocket. "My father was Ukrainian and proud of it. So—Stepan. Is there more of that?"

"Yeah. I made it this morning. Fresh."

Uncle Herman came in the back door just as Stepan was reaching for the vodka bottle he kept in the freezer. It was a premium Polish brand, an expensive indulgence for himself alone.

"How can you wear that hat in this weather?" Stepan asked the old man. "It must be close to ninety out there, hottest October on record, I heard. Where's your Panama?"

"Lost it. Blew away." Uncle Herman ran his thumb along the hat brim before hanging his fedora on its nail by the door. "This one's better. Fits right." He watched Stepan splash a shot of vodka into his lemonade. Uncle Herman didn't drink anymore but tried to keep his disapproval to himself.

Not well enough. Stepan felt suddenly awkward. He made a show of filling the ice cube tray, tilting the thing from side to side to level out the water. Of course, he spilled some before sliding the tray into the freezer. He stooped with an involuntary grunt to wipe the floor.

"Quit that groaning," Uncle Herman said from the living room doorway. "You don't get to do that until you pass eighty."

8

Hungary, 1955. For Stepan, the reference evoked only the vaguest memories, a *chiaroscuro* of images, each distinct but unconnected to the others. Light and dark. No sequence, no narrative, nothing to hold onto or properly recall.

Except for music. Father's viola, Mother's oboe, sometimes accompanied by friends with flutes, violins, a cello. He loved to watch their faces, serious but also relaxed, communicating to each other with a glance, a nod, a quick tap of the foot. There was coffee in small cups, plum brandy. Laughter. Music was the constant in his early years; it was, too, the bridge to a new life.

What else? A bowl of purloined apricots on the table, glowing in a glass bowl pierced by sunlight, plucked from a neighbor's tree under cover of sudden summer rain. The tree soon to fall to the ax of a tyrant determined to leave nothing standing that could bring people sustenance or joy.

And this: the smell of rubber and metal on the floor of his father's car, the hiss of tires against the road sending a delicious shiver of adventure through him, his body flattened behind the seats under blankets and coats. "Not a peep," Father had warned. "Or we're all in trouble." The impenetrable darkness that even now, as a man of fifty, he strove to recreate by pulling the bed covers over his head when he slept alone. He could sometimes achieve a momentary facsimile of that excitement edged with fear, but it was nothing like what he had felt as a child. *Nothing ever is, Stepan*, he admitted.

He hadn't thought about any of this until Lily started with her questions.

"Where you from, anyway?" she had demanded, less than a month after she joined the household.

"Why?" He was measuring tea leaves into his ceramic pot, the one with violets that matched his dishes. "Who wants to know?"

Lily looked around the kitchen, making a show of checking under the table. "Me. You see anybody else here? It's the way you talk. Like a Brit, kind of, but not really. Just weird."

Stepan poured in boiling water and covered the teapot with a towel. He shaved a circle off a cut lemon, dropped it into his cup. "I was born in Hungary, Szeged, in the south, near Yugoslavia," he said. "During the Soviet occupation. 1950. My parents..."

"No shit! Hungary? That's so cool. They had a revolution and everything. I read it in the encyclopedia."

"That was later, in 1956. And it failed. I was saying—" He stopped to pour tea into his cup, filling the room with mint and lemon aroma. "—my parents were musicians with a city opera company. Not a big one, but good enough to tour other Soviet bloc countries. Want some tea?"

"No, I only drink coffee. What?" she bristled at the amusement on his face. "I'm old enough! What was it like in Hungary, with the Russians and all?"

"I was a child. When you're little, everything just is, you have nothing to compare it to. My mother complained about living in only two rooms, after the country house she was used to, but their work was considered necessary, and they were good at it."

"Wait. Didn't people, like, suffer? That's all you hear about communists, like what monsters they are."

"People suffered and struggled and died, in prisons and work camps, hiding in cellars, first from the Nazis, then from the secret police. We were lucky, I guess, because even dictators like music, or at least understand how to use it to control the masses. Give people a piece of bread and a concert in the park and they'll keep working without making too much trouble."

Uncle Herman came in from his afternoon walk. He hung his hat on the nail behind the door and dropped a bundle of mail on the table. "You two got nothing to do?"

Lily got up, drained her coffee and washed the cup. "Can we go to the library tomorrow? I want to use the computer."

"No school?"

"It's Columbus Day, but the library's open half a day. I checked."

"I can drop her off in the morning," Stepan offered. "If you can pick her up later."

Uncle Herman nodded. "What's for dinner?"

"Pork chops. Want to eat with us, Stepan?"

"Thanks, kid," Stepan's smile was apologetic. "Another time. I've got a date."

Stepan preferred frozen food or takeout when he ate at home, which was rare. He had a fondness for fresh fruit, though, and kept a bowl of whatever was in season on the table, the way his mother had when he was a boy. Uncle Herman left it alone. He didn't believe in fruit, except maybe as a wedge of apple pie he could get at the diner if he felt like it.

They watched Uncle Herman go into the bathroom. From where she sat, Lily could see him through the open door. He stood at the window, hands clasped behind his back, peering over the half-curtain at the birds whose cheeping and squawking carried clearly through the autumn air. She turned back to Stepan.

"So why did you leave, if things weren't so bad for you?"

"Because, my dear, people need more than bread and a concert in the park, more even than a job. Because dictators and those who think like them and work for them, *are* monsters. You get tired of suspicious neighbors, of being afraid to say anything, of having nothing to read you can believe or think about. Of seeing people disappear and wondering who will be next, and why."

He stopped talking and looked at her, this skinny kid with her spiky two-tone hair, her thin wrists and large capable hands, her busy mind and many, many questions. How long had it been since he'd talked to anyone about this? How long since anyone had asked? This date tonight, would she care about anything more than the value of her dinner, about whether the price of the champagne he added to her glass was a fair trade for her compliance, her side of the bargain? And him, would he care? Or would the usual banter be enough, the empty words they both knew led only as far as the hotel room bed, paid for in advance, no need to stop at the desk.

He stood, took his teapot and cup to the sink.

"I'll do that," Lily said, but he ignored her, shook the tea leaves into the trash and washed up.

"They left because they could," he said without turning around. "My mother was red-haired, pretty, petite. Persuasive. She packed her best dishes, these—" he held up the teapot, dried it with care and put it away. "She convinced the border guards they were a wedding gift for her sister in Sarajevo, where—" he raised two fingers to indicate quotation marks, "'—we have a concert tomorrow night. The rest of the orchestra is on the train,' she said. 'We were too late, but look, here is our travel permit, the concert date, and also my sister's address. You see?' And she smiled sweetly, I'm sure."

"Wow. This is like one of those movies, with the old-time hats and those, you know, those shoes with funky heels."

"Isn't it? But it's all true. Mother could charm anyone; she kept the guards talking and laughing, so they wouldn't find me there behind the seat, under the blanket."

"Why'd they hide you?"

"You couldn't cross the border as a family. Kids stayed behind as insurance, to make sure the parents came back."

He told her the rest, about Yugoslavia, Czechoslovakia, getting passed from one courageous stranger to the next, expecting betrayal that, miraculously, never came. Then Vienna, Hamburg, London.

"So that's why you talk funny," Lily said. "Wow. And the dishes..."

Stepan looked down at her, bemused and silent, arms crossed over his chest. He sighed. "That's why," he said after a moment.

Uncle Herman stood in the doorway, scowling. "I know you twenty-five, thirty years. You never told me any of that."

"You never asked."

"Huh." He fixed Lily with a stare and waved at the mail on the table. "You got a letter."

9

The letter from her grandmother was just a note, the script large and loopy, the words shaky, uneven. *How are you getting on with Uncle Herman? Take care of yourself. These came for you.* Lily knew that since the year before, when the tremors started, Stella had given up writing in favor of the telephone. It wouldn't get better, the doctor said, but it didn't seem to be getting worse either. Lily had felt only a twinge of guilt on leaving her alone now that she was old. Grams had friends her age and a trusted doctor, who understood the progress of her changing needs, and she, Lily, had something important to do.

Besides, they had started to get on each other's nerves; Lily strained against rules that seemed to her an arbitrary harness, meant to rein in her suddenly urgent need for greater freedom and fewer questions. And Stella's heart palpitations, stoked by her fretful disposition, grew ever more frequent. *You'll feel better when I'm not around to make you crazy,* Lily had written on the page ripped from her notebook propped on the windowsill in her room. She figured Grams would have no reason to suspect anything until she was late getting home. She said she was spending the night with a friend, which gave her a day's head start on the cross-country bus.

How was she getting on with Uncle Herman? He was a cranky old bear, but that didn't bother her much. She was no ray of sunshine herself, most days. She couldn't figure, though, what made him so close-mouthed, as if it hurt him to grunt more than two words at a time.

Well, maybe it did.

Grams had told her about all those dead brothers and sisters and all, but somehow the loss hadn't made her grandmother wacky—she was friendly and talkative and liked to be among people. She had card club and book group and never missed a library movie night or Saturday lunch at the senior community center. Did she use people like a shield against memory, while Uncle Herman pulled himself in, giving nothing away?

And what was the deal with the birdwatching, the old man rooted at the bathroom window until somebody insisted on using the toilet? That was strange. Sometimes, in passing, she heard him talk to himself, naming the birds—chickadee, wren, titmouse, goldfinch—as if taking roll call, noting who showed up on time and who was absent, which seeds they liked. Weird.

And Nora. Who was she? A sweetheart, a lover, a crush who had finally broken his heart beyond repair? Maybe the answer to his odd behavior lay in finding out. *Fat chance of that,* she thought. *Is hell freezing over yet?*

The envelope from Stella held two postcards along with the note. The first showed a market scene: men in loose robes and round caps, with clay pots and carpets to sell, next to women seated behind mounds of fruit and colorful spices. In the foreground, a woman balanced a basket big as a prize pumpkin on her head, a baby wrapped in orange cloth tied to her back. How do they do that? Lily decided to try it at the first opportunity, when no one was around to see. The basket on the head thing, that is. Not the baby.

The back read:

> Hemp. Name for a tall annual herb (Cannabis sativa). The fiber is used for various kinds of cordage, also used in

making paper, cloth, and other products. The female flowering tops are used medicinally and are the source of the narcotics MARIJUANA and HASHISH. Hemp seed is used as bird food, and the oil is used in the manufacture of paints, varnishes, and soap. The true hemp plant, a member of the mulberry family, is related to the hop, which is used in making beer.

>Yours truly

There was no drawing this time, as if he guessed she already knew what weed looked like. The message was longer than usual, the writing smaller than ever, every bit of space covered with words.

She shook her head and looked at the second card. An ocean liner. Not one of those huge fancy ones with multiple decks and throngs of happy travelers; this one was relatively small, SS ITALIA painted on the life preserver attached below the railing. A lone man in a long overcoat stood holding the handrail, feet apart for balance, a swell of gray water rising at his back. Lily tried to make out the face, but the figure was too far away, his features obscured by the brim of his hat. The card looked old, the edges yellowed, the black-and-white picture like something out of a war movie. A photograph, not a postcard. Lily turned it over.

> Odysseus. In Greek mythology, son and successor of King Laertes of Ithaca. A leader of Greek forces during the Trojan War, Odysseus was noted for his cunning strategy and his wise counsel. In post-Homeric legend, however, he was pictured as a wily, lying, and evil man. The legends of Odysseus' wanderings have been used throughout literature, most notably in the Odyssey.

> Yours truly

Around the text, her father had sketched several pigs, the

expressions on their upturned faces ranging from puzzlement to rage to blank stupidity. "I get it, Dad," she smirked. "Nice work." She knew about the sailors who were changed into swine while Odysseus fooled around with the witch Circe. She had read it in Uncle Herman's *Britannica*. But who, exactly, was wily, lying, and evil? She wondered if the man in the photograph was a relative, someone disreputable, on the lam.

She showed it to Uncle Herman. "Who is this? Do you know him?"

He squinted at it and shrugged. "Nope."

Lily frowned. Another dead end, then. Was she looking for meaning where there was none? Maybe there was no puzzle except in her mind.

Neither card was signed. Both carried the usual *Columbia Encyclopedia* attribution. She had them in her hand, to add to the ones in her cookie tin, when she remembered to check the postmark APO zip code. 10996. West Point. "Hot dog," she said and looked up to meet Stepan's questioning gaze. "He's still here."

10

"Who?" Stepan dried his hands and hung the towel on the rack. "Who's still here?"

Lily didn't answer right away. She put the cards down on the table, turned them over and studied the images again. Uncle Herman moved toward the door, the rest of the mail tucked under his arm.

"I might as well tell you, right? You too, Uncle Herman." She sighed. "I came here to find my father."

"Here?" Stepan spread his arms to encompass the room, the house.

"No, not *here*. I knew he wouldn't be *here*." She gave a sad little laugh. "That's too easy, and also nuts. I meant here at West Point."

"Why? Is he expecting you?"

"No, Stepan, he's not. He just keeps sending me these goofy encyclopedia cards. He doesn't even sign them. Like it's some kind of game, only he forgot to tell me the rules."

Uncle Herman half-turned in the doorway. "Stella told me about the cards. What makes you think he's here?"

She flipped the market scene over and pointed. "Look. The APO address. There's a code that tells you where he's serving—Europe or Asia, or, if there's a zip code, which US base. I looked it up on the library computer. See? 10996. That's West Point." She sat down and repeated, "He's here in New York, at West Point. That's why I came."

Stepan shook his head. "I'm confused. Have you talked to

him? Does he know you're here?"

"The last time he saw me I was ten days old. So no, I don't think he knows I'm here, do you?" Lily snorted and tossed the cards on the table.

"Then why..." Stepan looked from Lily to Uncle Herman, who stared at the floor.

"Because. I want to know what kind of man runs out on his own little baby—and I know that's not so unusual, so don't even say that. But why pester me with this guessing game, these random cards and stupid messages? Like he's invented some kind of cool new homeschooling program." Lily swiped at her eyes, angry at the unwelcome tears. "He can't love me, 'cause he doesn't know me. Who knows why he's afraid to sign his name. And he is afraid, right? I mean, who the fuck says Yours Truly anymore? That's so... so..." she struggled for the word, "...so Dickens!" She snatched the towel off the rack and wiped her face. "I want to know, is all." She hiccupped and blew her nose.

"People walk away. Who knows why? If you want to go, go. Don't whine about it." Uncle Herman left the kitchen, then added from the darkness of the living room, "Put that towel in the laundry."

Stepan picked up the two cards, took a long time reading the messages. "So this is why you're always at the *Britannica*," he said almost to himself.

Lily gasped. "What? No!" She stared at the towel balled up in her fist. "Is it?"

"Maybe on some level you're having a conversation." Stepan looked at her kindly. "I don't know."

38

11

In November Lily called her grandmother to ask for tips on preparing the Thanksgiving meal. "I know what to do, pretty much. I'm just not sure about the stuffing. We're having a breast, not a whole bird."

Stella recited the instructions. "But you do know what to do," she confirmed. "Just bake the stuffing in a separate pan and baste everything every twenty minutes."

"Thanks, Grams. Sometimes I think I could serve them any old thing—a sponge with gravy—to see if they would notice. Which they would. That's dumb. Forget I said that. Anyway, I figure since I'm a freeloader here, the least I can do is make some good food, right?"

"You're not a freeloader. Your father sends me money every month; I share some with your uncle, for your expenses. The rest goes into your savings account. You'll need it later, cupcake."

"For me? He sends money for me? Since when? You never told me."

She listened to her grandmother's breathing. It wasn't labored, exactly, but not normal either. It came through the telephone connection like a presence, audible as a sigh, familiar and a little sad. She scanned the room, noticed as if for the first time how dark everything was: the dull brown carpet, mahogany bookcase, black leather chairs; even the plaid sofa was in subdued autumnal shades. She pictured Stella far away in her living room, saw the crocheted doily under the phone, lacy curtains freshly starched every six months, pastel upholstery accented with rose and turquoise pillows. *Could two people from the same family be less alike? And where do I fit in?*

Her eyes returned to the bookcase, its matched set of forest green Harvard classics; the black-bound *Britannica*; Webster's *Unabridged Dictionary* in dingy beige cloth covers; Audubon's *Birds of North America* and Jansen's *History of Art* in gray; all eleven volumes of Will and Ariel Durant's *Story of Civilization*, their colorful dust jackets lending a touch of relief to the somber surroundings.

"Well, Lily," Stella said. "Did I answer all your questions? If there's nothing else..."

"Wait. Grams, when you moved to California, did you and Uncle Herman argue about who got to keep the *Britannica*? I mean, it belongs to both of you, right?"

Stella laughed. "Oh, no, dear. We argued, but not about that. It would have been too much trouble and expense to cart those books across the country. And anything I needed to know I could find in the library, couldn't I. So no, we didn't even talk about it, much less argue. Why do you ask?"

"No reason. I wondered, is all." She yawned. "It's pretty cool, you know. I've been reading it."

"Have you? Well, good. That's what it's for. Hi, Margrit," Stella said, her voice fading as she turned away from the receiver. "I'll be right there. I'm just talking to Lily."

"You go ahead, Grams. Thanks. Tell Margrit I said hi."

"Oh, I just remembered. The only time I missed those fact books was when your father was ten or so and asked if we could have an encyclopedia at home, like some of his friends did. Well, I was alone by then, you know, I couldn't afford a big set like that. So he found a book in a used bookstore, a fat book with tiny print that had everything in it. He pestered me until I bought it. Ten dollars. But he was happy. I don't remember what it was called. Some kind of encyclopedia."

"Columbia?" Lily prompted, now wide awake. "Go have your coffee, Grams."

"Yes, Columbia. Yes. Always had his nose in it, reading me this or that while I did the cooking or ironing. He loved that book so much he took it with him when he enlisted." Stella chuckled. "Don't worry about the dinner, it will be good. I go now. Margrit brought brownies."

Columbia Encyclopedia. Lily hung up the phone and sat motionless. Her head buzzed with half-formed questions. What had drawn her to the *Britannica*, why did she keep returning to its pages, scanning its entries? Was this some kind of psychic legacy, some peculiar genetic connection to the father she didn't know? Or a simple coincidence, with no more meaning than hair color, say, or height, or some inherited allergy?

And the money. What about the money?

She listened to Uncle Herman in the kitchen, the rustle of a paper bag. She heard him put canned goods away in the cabinet and start a pot of coffee. "Damn," she said, looking up when he came into the living room. "I forgot to ask Grams for her apple pie recipe. I don't know how she makes it so good."

12

"What kind of tunes do you like, Uncle Herman? Like, oldies, or those, you know, big band numbers with girls in sparkly dresses?" Lily tugged at a strip of crisp turkey skin with her fingers, detaching it from the meat left on the platter.

The old man shot her a look. "Don't pick at the food. Didn't your grandmother teach you manners?"

"Yeah, she did. I figured you wouldn't care." She looped the skin around her fork and put it in her mouth. "Oh, wait," she said, chewing. "I bet you go for that classical stuff, Beethoven's Fifth and all that. Am I right?"

Stepan refilled his wine glass. "That's what I was raised on. My parents, it was their whole world. All their friends were either musicians or poets. Or both."

Uncle Herman frowned at the all but empty wine bottle. "You drank all that?"

"I helped a little," Lily giggled and drained her glass. She wanted more but didn't dare ask.

"That was one of your better ideas." Uncle Herman glared at Stepan. "You know she's not even fifteen."

"Come on, Herman, it's a holiday. Don't tell me you didn't get a sip now and then at the family dinner table." He raised his glass. "That's for the great dinner, kid. You deserve it. Hard to believe it's your first time."

"What, the wine? No, not really, if you want to know. Oh!" She clapped a hand over her mouth. "You mean the whole

43

Thanksgiving thing. Yeah, first time by myself. It's pretty easy, though, no big deal. Except for the pie."

They fell silent. Lily eyed another strip of turkey skin but didn't need another reprimand. She buttered the last biscuit and gave Stepan half. Took a bite.

She didn't want the biscuit. She wanted to understand about families. Mothers. Fathers. People who knew where they belonged, and who with. People who stuck around and took care of you. This dinner, this holiday tradition, always made her feel she'd crashed the party, trespassed on seats reserved for ticket holders only. Back home, her grandmother had tried; she cooked the meal, invited a neighbor or a friend from work as if to fill the space left by the missing. Maybe she felt it too. She must have—how could you not miss your own son, or all those brothers and sisters? Or maybe she was used to it, all those people gone long ago, she and Uncle Herman left to finish growing up on their own. How long did it take to get used to it?

Lily shook her head. *Stop that*, she told herself. Uncle Herman was family and Stepan, well, it looked like he had nowhere else to go. *Deal with it, crybaby.*

Uncle Herman turned sideways on his chair and stretched out his legs. His legs looked thin, too thin to fill the worn denim of his jeans, the knees sharp, bony. He reached into his shirt pocket for a toothpick.

Stepan looked down at his plate. He hadn't meant to bring up not one but two sore subjects in the space of a single careless remark. *Don't tell me you didn't get a nip now and then at the family dinner table.* Herman had stopped drinking years before they'd met, but Stepan gathered it had been extreme, bordering on self-destructive. He only heard about the family tragedies through vague remarks, sketchy references with no details. Herman wouldn't talk about those losses, and Stepan had stopped asking.

Stepan wondered if maybe now he'd gone too far. He wanted to say, *I'm sorry, I'm an idiot, I drank too much wine,* but the words wouldn't come. It was best to drop it. He would only make it worse, and Uncle Herman didn't seem to care. Stepan smoothed the mashed potatoes left on his plate with his knife, pressed the tines of his fork in to make lines and pushed baby peas in at random in between.

Lily laughed, breaking the tension. "Hey, what is that, pea music?"

"Potato mash-up serenade," Stepan answered. He leaned back in his chair while she collected the plates and scraped his creation into the trash.

"So, Uncle Herman," she said over her shoulder, swishing hot suds in the dishpan. "What kind of music? You never said."

"No kind. Birdsong." Uncle Herman shifted the toothpick to the corner of his mouth with his tongue. "No music."

"Wow, really?" She unfurled a length of aluminum wrap and covered the carved-up turkey breast, folding the excess foil in to make a tight package. "How come?"

"No reason. Don't need it, don't like it." He stood to help clear the table. Stepan sat sipping his wine, nibbling his biscuit.

"I guess that's why there's, like, no stereo in your house. Not even a cassette player for my tapes."

Uncle Herman pushed his chair in. "Yep. Move over, I'll wash. You could help, Prince Charming." He tossed Stepan a dishtowel.

Stepan didn't like cleaning up. Except for rinsing his teapot and cup, which he didn't trust to anyone else's hands, he wasn't in the habit. Growing up, it wasn't expected of him. Go read a book, his mother would say. Play a record. Now his own meals came with disposable containers; about the only dishes he used were that teapot and cup. Moving slowly, with obvious reluctance, he picked up the saucer that served as a butter dish. Lily was stashing the rest of the leftovers. "What tapes?" he said to her back. "What are kids listening to now?"

"Oh, the new stuff's all crap." She took the butter from him and put it away. "Before I left, I found some tapes in our basement, in a shoebox. Get this," she squeaked, looking up at him. "You know what kind of shoes? Birkenstocks! Hippie shoes." She half-closed her eyes and drawled, "Some trip, man. Wild." They both laughed. Even Uncle Herman cracked a smile.

"Anyway, the tapes were my mother's, Grams said. Really cool stuff from, like, the eighties. Talking Heads. David Byrne, he's the best, so not about rules, or stupid romance. And Annie Lennox, you know her? She's even cooler, 'cause she's a chick. And Cyndi Lauper, and the Thompson Twins. The Police. The Clash. Pink Floyd." She lowered her voice and intoned, "We don't need no... ed-u-cation..."

Lily ran off to her room, came back with the box and dumped a dozen or more cassettes out on the table. "Look. There's even some *really* old stuff. Dylan, Janis, the Stones, and—check this out—the Beach Boys. You know? The Beach Boys!" She sat down. "But I can't listen to them."

Uncle Herman rinsed out the roasting pan and drained the dishwater. "Radio still works."

"Oh, Uncle Herman," Lily sighed. "It's not the same. You can't get any good stations here, only that super-lame pop garbage, and country. Ugh." She shuddered. "Or that, whaddyacallit, Christian Rock. I don't know if it's really Christian, but it sure ain't Rock. Radio's so bad around here, I'd rather listen to NPR. Just kidding," she added quickly and giggled. Stepan, dish towel in hand, stood smiling broadly. Whether at her taste, her musical assessment, or her enthusiasm, she couldn't tell.

Uncle Herman switched on the coffee maker. "How's about that pie?"

"I'm telling you, it's a disaster. The filling's kinda runny, and it's not sweet enough, and the crust, well... Grams always made the pie. I need more practice." For a moment, Lily looked small and sad.

"We got ice cream," Uncle Herman said. "Good with everything."

They ate the pie, drank the coffee. Both men scraped every last crumb off their plates, and Uncle Herman even took a second slice. "Go call your grandmother," he said when they were done. "Wish her a happy."

13

Uncle Herman didn't come down for breakfast on Monday. Lily heard him in the attic, pushing boxes around, maybe even furniture. She'd never been up there; it was off-limits. She was about to call up a third time when he stuck his head out over the pull-down ladder and said, "I can get my own food. Go to school."

It stung. Lily tried to tell herself it didn't matter, that he was a crusty old character not used to being around other people, but it still stung. She skipped the bus and walked, head lowered into a frigid wind. "Feel like goddam Snow White around here," she muttered, tugging her cap down tightly around her ears. "Good thing there's only two of them. Seven would probably kill me."

She pulled her parka collar closer against the icy rain, jammed her reddened hands into her pockets. Her face felt too numb to cry. *Just wait until I find my father,* she thought. *You'll miss me then.* Would it kill the old man to talk to her like a... a human being once in a while? She was tired of his snapping and growling like you'd be doing him a favor if you just dropped dead or disappeared. And Stepan. He'd left right after Thanksgiving without a word, making it clear you weren't important enough to know where he was going or when he'd be back. At least he was polite when he was home. When he noticed her.

Lily surrendered to the weather and caught a passing bus. She sat alone on the back bench, letting her mind swing to self-pity when it wasn't planning revenge. She knew how to be rude, too. She'd cook her own dinner and eat it right in front of them. Slowly.

"Idiot," she said to the frosted window. "Who will care? Nobody." Stepan would go out, and Uncle Herman had enough canned corned beef hash stashed away to last until Memorial Day.

Uncle Herman was coming down the attic ladder when she got home in the afternoon. "Were you up there all day?" she couldn't help asking, watching him back down one careful step at a time. She had tried to stay mad but had felt her anger pivot in history class, right after lunch. Goddam Nazis. She was sick of hearing about them. Wasn't there anything else to learn about, like China, maybe, or India, or other places she'd read about in the *Britannica*? Australia. Japan. But no, it seemed like if you were the worst possible person anyone could ever be, people would talk about you forever.

She tried to hold on to the morning's resentment, to say to her great-uncle, "Doesn't your skinny ass have anything better to do than poke around that crappy attic all day?" But she couldn't do it, Grams hadn't raised her that way. "Watch it!" she cried out when his foot nearly missed a step and his carpet slipper plopped to the floor.

He swayed to one side but held on; the electrical cord from the gray plastic box under his arm spiraled wildly through the air. Lily picked up the slipper and held it to her chest, not daring to breathe until the old man had both feet on the floor.

"Too much junk up there," he said. "Couldn't find it the first time. Had to go out for thistle seed anyway. For the goldfinches." He put the box down on the kitchen table and held his hand out for the slipper.

"Oh, here," Lily laid it on the floor between them. "Like, what kind of junk?" Everything in Uncle Herman's house was old, but there wasn't much of it. What would he have hidden away, and why?

He bent down to pull his sock up and poke his foot into his shoe. "Stuff. Hats, shoes. Dresses. Pictures. Too much." He straightened. Lily looked into his clouded eyes.

Too much what? Too much stuff, or time, or memory, or pain? She wanted desperately to know, but his look said, don't ask.

Why couldn't people just say things? Why all the hints and clues and riddles? She didn't think every kid's life was this kind of idiotic guessing game, where nobody straight-out told you anything, keeping you in the dark about things that really mattered, like who they were and how they got that way. Where they'd been. Who they loved.

"What's that?" She pointed to the box on the table.

He turned it over, wiped the dust off the top with the hem of his shirt. "Cassette player," he said. "Don't you know? Go get a tape, try it. Not a good one," he added. "Might get ruined."

Lily ran to her room and came back with the shoe box. She rummaged through her tape stash, trying to decide which one she could live without, when Uncle Herman said, "Never mind. There's one in there." He plugged the thing in, blew some more dust out of the crevices around the controls, sat down and pressed Play.

There was a whirring, scratchy sound then, suddenly, music. "Oh," Lily exclaimed. "Grams likes that. It's big band, right?" She moved around the room, shaking her head and swinging her hips, snapping her fingers to the brassy beat. She struck a pose and faced Uncle Herman. "That's so cool..." she started to say, and fell silent. His gnarly hands were folded one over the other, his face a melancholy mask, the lines around his mouth stony. "Uncle Herman," she said.

51

All at once the music slowed, the sound stretched and whined and stopped. Uncle Herman turned the machine off and ejected the tape. It came out in a tangled, loopy mess, looking like a celluloid bird's nest when he put it on the table.

They stared at it in silence. Lily was the first to speak. "Nora?"

He didn't answer right away, bent down to unravel the tape, turning the sprocket with a pencil to wind the loose part back onto the spindle. "It's broken." He held up two loose ends. "No good."

He stood up, pressing both fists into the table as he rose, like an old, old man. Lily watched him walk slowly to the trash can in the corner by the back door and let the cassette fall into it. "She liked to dance," he said without turning around.

"With you?" Lily tried to imagine Uncle Herman with younger bones and muscles, not so hidebound or surly. Capable of joy. Holding Nora in his arms or swinging with her, fingers entwined, feet flashing, keeping the beat. Groovin' to the music, to each other.

Or not. She sees Nora turn up the volume on the cassette player. *Dance with me!* Uncle Herman smiling, maybe, shaking his head. Nora shimmies across the kitchen, unpartnered, her face showing more determination than pleasure. He looks on, bemused, leaves the room before the music stops.

What happened between them? Did he let Nora walk away, too rigid in his outlook, too stubborn, frozen by fear of happiness or any kind of feeling? Love most of all. It wasn't the dancing, but then again, maybe it was. People got hung up on all kinds of strange things—postcards and birds.

Uncle Herman ignored Lily's question. After a while, he unplugged the cassette player and moved it to the end of the kitchen counter. "I can fix it," he said. "Tomorrow. Needs cleaning."

Lily spread her math homework out on the kitchen table. She heard him in his room—the sound of his dry cough carried clearly through the thin wall. Outside, the wind picked up, the room grew chilly. On her way to get a sweatshirt from her closet, she saw him standing at the bathroom window, watching the birds.

Why had he done that? He knew better than anyone what kind of tape would be in the machine. And he'd turned it on deliberately, on purpose. Why? Had he been testing himself, measuring the thickness of the scab over his wound, to see if it would hold, if he could take it? Or was he telling her something, in his peculiar way, something he couldn't bring himself to say but had grown tired of carrying around. Where? In his memory, his bones, his heart? What did he want from her, what was her part in this charade?

Back in the kitchen, she stared blankly at the geometry printout. The problems weren't difficult, but her mind was elsewhere. Did she really need details, stories, pictures, explanations? Maybe not. Maybe right now it was enough for her that Nora, whoever she was, had occupied these rooms, this kitchen at the very least; that she had used vanilla and nutmeg and bay leaves, had filled this space in Uncle Herman's life with aromatic essences and sometimes, music.

Maybe one day Lily would see that woman's shoes, shake the dust out of those dresses, try on the hats and gloves. She was sure there would be gloves, even if Uncle Herman hadn't said so. And that would be grand, as Grams liked to say. But for now, she felt she understood enough. *I'm just a kid,* she thought. *How much more do I need to know?*

She took the extra chair, the one against the wall behind the table, the one no one ever used. In the bathroom, she nudged her great-uncle to one side and placed the chair in front of the window.

"Here." She parted the half-curtains a few inches in the middle. "Sit down."

14

How could anyone hate music? That was something Lily could not understand. "I mean, everybody likes some kind of tunes," she said to Stepan. "Or maybe some people don't care what they listen to, it's all okay by them. But what's to hate?"

Stepan grunted and turned a page in his publisher's catalog. "Look at this." He jabbed the book cover illustration with his finger. "More semiotics. Nobody buys this stuff, nobody cares. They should just sell it directly to libraries and universities and be done with it." He sighed as if already exhausted by the prospect of presenting such esoteric material to his bookstore clients. "Your Uncle Herman, he's an odd duck. Maybe he was listening to, I don't know, Slavonic dances or Neapolitan love songs or Charlie Parker when his parents' house burned down. Or maybe it has something to do with Nora."

"Again. Who's this Nora? What's the freakin' mystery?" Lily closed the MAR-MUS volume of the *Britannica* and reached for the RUT-SEP one farther along the shelf. She turned toward the back of the book and scanned the entries.

"He's never said much about her, as long as I've known him. I gather she's someone from his past, a lover, maybe, or a fiancée. I've wondered too, but he won't say, and we probably shouldn't ask. A man has a right to his secrets."

"Huh. And a woman doesn't?"

"I never said that."

"Yeah, you did. You implied it." Lily glared at him.

"Okay, a person then. A person has a right to keep a secret. Better?" He met her stare with a sly little smile.

She was silent a while, her finger tracing headings in the encyclopedia. "Here it is. Semiotics. Sounds kinda cool, but I guess most people would rather read something else, like you say."

"As," Stepan corrected. "As you say."

Lily's face darkened, the scowl spreading from suddenly angry eyes to a grimly set jaw. "AS," she repeated.

"What?" Stepan looked bewildered. "Don't you want to talk like the smart kid you are?"

"I hate, HATE being a kid. Somebody's always telling you what to do, like you don't have a brain." She flung the book aside. "Oh, sorry. I meant AS."

"As if, actually," Stepan said softly. "Don't get mad. I just want to help."

"Yeah, well. Everybody wants to HELP. Or help themselves. They look at you like you're their personal hamburger, put their paws on you whenever they want."

Stepan put his catalog on the floor. He rose and walked to the window, contemplated the patch of browned grass between their house and the next one, hands in his pockets. "Lily," he said, his back to her. "What happened? Was it after you ran away?"

Lily sniffed loudly, he turned and looked at her. She sat, stiff, feet planted flat on the floor, one sock blue striped, the other black, both with holes in the toe. She stuck her chin out at him, red-faced, her cheeks tear-stained but eyes defiant.

Stepan went into the kitchen and filled a glass with water. She took it from him but did not drink. He sat down in his chair and waited.

"It was the second night out, before Grams even knew I was gone. Montana, Wyoming, I don't remember. I was in the bus stop waiting room, sleeping on a bench. Woke up with some creep bending over me, his hand on my ass." She gripped the glass hard enough to make the water quiver and drip down the side. "Not some smelly old dude either. Business suit, tie sticking out of his coat pocket, briefcase on the floor. Booze breath. Boner big as a fucking banana in his pants."

"Was anybody else around?"

"Just a homeless lady in the corner, out for the count. Ticket window closed. Four o'clock in the morning, next bus east not due until 5:51, according to the timetable. I mean, was I screwed, or what?"

"Lily..." Stepan said and stopped.

"Well, I wasn't going down that easy. I swung my backpack and decked him a good one. You shoulda seen his face! 'Easy, girlie,' he mumbled. 'I was just, you know, lonely.' 'Go play with your balls,' I said. 'If you have any.'" She giggled, slurped some water, and set the glass on the coffee table. "It had rained some, the bench outside the building was wet. But I sat out there and waited for the bus, 'cause it felt safer to be out in the open than inside with that dipshit. I couldn't sleep, though. Saw my first sunrise ever."

"Did he bother you again?"

"Nah. You know how bullies are. Can't let them see you're scared."

"Were you? Scared?"

"What do you think? Like, shitless. He could do whatever. Nothing to stop him but my big mouth. Anyway, after a while the ticket guy showed up, all official-looking in his little blue coat and conductor's cap. So, I caught a coupla zzs but didn't really sleep until the bus. I knew enough to sit right up front."

"I'm sorry..."

"Why are you sorry? Actually, he looked like you, a little.

What was it they used to call you salesmen—commercial travelers? I read that in a book once. And all your *dates*. What's that about?"

"I've never forced anyone," Stepan bristled. "You make it sound shady. I'm not ashamed of what I do, nor of my lifestyle, either."

"Okay, okay. I take it back. Anyway, he was the worst one. Most of them just look at you with those, you know, those eyes. Like they've just escaped prison camp and you're the first woman they've seen in half a century. Or they sit next to you on the bus, push their hammy thigh up against your leg, pretending to be asleep. Gimme a break. Men are pathetic."

15

Lily picked up the encyclopedia. "Anyway. Semiotics," she read out. "*A general theory of signs and symbolism, usually divided into the branches of pragmatics, semantics, and syntactics.* What the hell does that mean? No, don't tell me. I'll look it up."

She pulled Uncle Herman's old *Webster's Unabridged* from the bookshelf, slid the water glass aside and laid the ten-pound dictionary on the coffee table.

"Careful," Stepan said. "Table could be wet."

Lily snorted. "Like anyone would notice." She ran one hand over the once-beige cloth cover, then lifted up the book and wiped the table with her sleeve. "There."

She flipped through the pages, stopping now and then to read an entry or examine a drawing. "There was one guy, a truck driver," she said, her tone casual, offhanded. "My money ran out in Indiana. I was broke. Hungry." She paused, her finger on the 'P' index notch. "I had already called Grams to tell her I was all right, so she wouldn't send out the Marines. I wasn't about to have her come rescue me. Nope. Eyes on the prize, like they say. AS they say. One way or another I was going to get here." She turned to 'P' and smoothed the page with her palm.

"So? The truck driver?" Stepan asked, his catalog, unopened, back on his lap.

"So I hitched, what else? This guy seemed okay, clean-cut, a Jesus Saves sticker on his dash. Like he needed a reminder, you know? We talked. I told him where I was going and why. Stuff I never told anybody, until you and Uncle Herman, but it seemed cool—he was friendly without being all in my business or giving me advice I didn't need. He told me about his wife, back home in Georgia, his dog, his new baby boy. Fourth one. 'I might could take you as far as Ohio,' he said. 'Then I'm headin' south.' He was polite, didn't try anything." Her finger stopped midway down the column of entries on the page. "Found it," she said.

"Finish the story," Stepan prompted. "I hear your Uncle Herman's car. I'd know that idle anywhere."

"Well, he bought me soup and a muffin in a diner. When we came out, he gave me a bus ticket to Cincinnati, a paper bag with a sandwich in it, plus one of those little milk cartons like you get in the school cafeteria. 'I hope you find your daddy all right. There's some bad people in the world,' he said. 'You take care.' *Don't I know it*, I thought. *Good thing you're not one of them.* But I just smiled and thanked him. Later, when I ate the sandwich, I found forty bucks underneath."

Stepan put his pen down. "Do you have any idea how lucky you are?"

"Yeah, whatever. Why shouldn't people be nice to each other? It's not hard. So here," she read. "*Pragmatics: branch of semiotics dealing with causal relations between words or symbols and their users...*" She made a face, skipped a few hundred pages. *Semantics: branch of semiotics dealing with relations between signs and what they denote.* And here, *Syntactics: branch of logic,* blah, blah, blah, *signs that occur...complete abstraction....*" Lily raised her eyebrows and pulled the corners of her mouth down in a clueless grimace. She and Stepan both laughed.

"Okay, I guess I don't need to know everything yet," she said.

"Think of it this way," Stepan tapped his catalog with two fingers. "Sometimes we use one thing to stand in for something else, even if we don't know we're doing it."

Lily looked up, her eyes wide. "You mean, like, symbols. Yeah, I get that. But these other things, syntactics and all. What's that about? Why does it matter?"

"It doesn't, really, unless you're a linguist or dabble in philosophy. You don't need to use complex language to understand basic concepts and how they apply to everyday life."

"Like what?"

"Like, say, semantics. It's just a high-flown way to talk about word choice or shades of meaning."

"So?"

"So, in some ways writing or speaking is like cooking. You consider your ingredients and choose the ones that combine well to create the desired result. You don't have to study the chemistry of baking to make a cake."

"Damn, you're smart," Lily said. "I never would have thought of that—like how you can jazz up a simple recipe with spices and stuff, or how different people use the same words to say something nobody ever said before. Damn." She closed the dictionary and returned it to the shelf.

"Yes. On the other hand," Stepan gestured like an orator, with the hint of a smile. "You can make yourself crazy trying to find meaning in disconnected events, looking for messages in ordinary, superficial things."

"Like my father's cards," Lily murmured. She sat back, crossed her arms on top of her head, fingers interlaced.

"Like your father's cards. Maybe there's symbolism in his choice of images or subject that he's not even aware of. Maybe it's, as you say, his eccentric idea of a game. Or he may be trying to fulfill his own interpretation of a parental role that makes him uncomfortable. Unable to openly acknowledge the obligation by using his name. Or yours."

"Maybe you're full of it," Uncle Herman said from the doorway. "People do what they do."

"Yeah." Lily sighed. "They do. Hi, Uncle Herman." She got up and headed for the kitchen. "Guess I'll go study some ingredients for dinner."

16

The only reason Uncle Herman had a TV at all was to watch nature programs and, now and then, a wrestling match.

He couldn't explain about the wrestling. Didn't have to. He liked the wordless grappling, the thudding satisfaction of seeing one man lift the other off the ground, send him crashing to the mat, and saunter off in sweaty grimacing glory. Not unlike rams butting heads, locking horns until the weaker one's legs buckled in defeat, and it was over. If he ever wondered what the silent ewes might be thinking, grinding their jaws like gum-chewing teenagers, waiting for the champion to escort them to the breeding grounds, he didn't let on. Did they have a preference? How much did it matter who won? And what about the loser? It looked like he simply limped away, consigned to a solitary existence outside the herd, content to watch birds squabble over seeds. He could have been more persistent, fought harder. But what good would that have done if the one he'd had his eye on had already walked away without waiting for the contest to end?

The three of them were in the darkened living room, while on the screen the Grinch shoved yet another Christmas tree up the chimney with diabolical glee. Uncle Herman sat in his armchair, the yellow light from the pole lamp trained on the newspaper held in front of his face. He was NOT watching some cartoon grump get his comeuppance from a bunch of starry-eyed do-gooders. He would do what he always did, evenings—sit in his chair and read his newspaper by the light of his lamp.

Watching TV had been Stepan's idea. "My favorite holiday program, *How the Grinch Stole Christmas,* is on tonight," he said after dinner. "As a kid, I hid the book under my bed rather than return it to the library. My mother finally bought me my own copy." He settled himself into the other chair, balanced his cup and saucer on the arm, and turned up the volume. "Maybe that's why we get along, Herman," he added. "You pretending you have no heart."

Uncle Herman bent back one corner of his newspaper and glared at Stepan. "Bullshit." He snapped the paper back in front of his face. "Who says we get along?"

Lily burrowed deeper into the corner of the couch. "That's not nice," she said. "He really has no heart. The Grinch, I mean. Not at first." She shivered, tucked her legs up, reached for the blanket draped across the back and pulled the frayed edge of the plaid up to her neck. There was no point asking Uncle Herman to turn up the heat. "Hey, Stepan. Ever since you told me your story, I can't get it out of my head." She paused. "So, what's it like?"

Stepan blew across the steaming cup in his hand, sending a whiff of rum-laced tea in her direction. "What, exactly?"

"Leaving, just like that, with some of your stuff and none of your friends. Your rooms, your—" She gestured vaguely at the shadowy surroundings. "You know, furniture, books, your favorite pillow. Your school or, I don't know, corner candy store. Your place. Like, never coming back."

"I was small. My world was defined by my parents, they protected me. As long as we were together, I felt fine."

"And you stayed together."

"Mostly. When they performed, I was allowed to be in the wings, among the stagehands, asleep in a chair as often as not."

He sipped his tea and leaned his head against the back of the chair. "There was one time.... My father left us for a few days. He came back, but even I noticed a change. He was nervous, irritable. Thinner. Let it be, he said to my mother, waving her questions away. Let it be! It was the only time I remember hearing him raise his voice to her."

"Wow. So he was, like, interrogated?"

"Probably. He never would talk about it, even when I was older. After a while, I stopped asking."

Uncle Herman rustled his paper. "Don't you know how it is to walk out and hit the road? Why you bothering him?"

Lily shifted on the couch, turning in his direction. "That's not the same! I'm not a refugee! I can go back if I want to, I can talk to Grams on the phone or write her a letter. And this place, with you two, feels a little strange sometimes, but it's not a foreign country. We speak the same language." She laughed. "Sort of. Want coffee?"

Uncle Herman turned the page. "Decaf."

She got up, draped the blanket over her shoulders, and came back with two mugs and a plate of cookies on a tray. "Anyway," she continued. "What I really want to know is how your parents felt when they ran off and nobody knew where they were. Like, their family, who stayed behind and couldn't visit or talk or write to them. I mean, when your parents left, they knew they'd be alone. Was it worth it, you think?"

"If you're wondering whether they missed their family, well, of course they did. Eventually, they made a new life, with good new friends and interesting work." He took his eyes off the screen and peered at her with a little smile. "But if you're thinking their flight was anything like your insane adventure, there's no comparison."

Lily stared at the TV, at the happy little creatures holding hands and singing, even though all their holiday trimmings had been taken away. She held her coffee with both hands and said nothing for a while, her jaw set hard. "I wasn't," she said finally. "That's not what I was thinking." *I want to know if my father misses me,* she wanted to say. *Why he would hold a grudge against a baby. If he's ever sorry he went away. If there's a special reason he doesn't want to be found.*

17

She took a cookie, broke it in two and dipped one piece in her cup. "Uncle Herman? Grams told me how everybody died, you know, in the war and all, and those freaky accidents. Bummer."

Uncle Herman studied her over the rim of his mug, the steam clouding his glasses so she couldn't see his eyes. He waited. "Yeah?"

"Well, I was wondering. How did your parents meet?"

He lowered the mug and cradled it on his lap, letting his newspaper fall over his knees. "On a ship," he said. "Why you want to know?"

"It's my family, right? I should know. Grams is younger than you, but she's starting to forget things." Lily picked up another cookie. "What ship? Was it like a cruise or something, with Bingo for the old folks and dancing after dinner?" She took a bite. "I saw that in a movie."

"How would I know? I wasn't there." Uncle Herman slurped his coffee. After a moment he said, "The *Majestic*. If you must know."

"Really? You have any pictures, like, in the attic?" She sat forward and looked at him expectantly from under raised eyebrows. "Never mind, I'll look it up tomorrow in the encyclopedia. So what happened?"

Uncle Herman sighed. "My father was a student, in Berlin. His parents were coming to visit for Christmas. In London they got a telegram from him, saying, *Don't come. Everybody sick. School closed.*"

"Wow. So then what happened? Grams said they died. Can you tell me?"

"Might as well, so you'll stop pestering me. My father met them in London and sailed back with them. Everybody got sick, the ship was full of it—"

"The flu, right? From Russia." Stepan interjected.

"Don't interrupt. Yeah, the flu from Russia. My father got better. The old folks died before the ship reached New York."

Lily grew quiet. "And your mother? Why was she there?"

"Questions, questions! She was traveling with her parents. A holiday, like you said. They caught it and died. She didn't."

As you said, she mouthed. She glanced at Stepan, but his eyes were fixed on the screen. "So, they got married. Romantic, huh? Grams told me their names, but I forgot."

"John and Clara." Uncle Herman put his mug down on the chairside table and picked up the newspaper. "Now leave me alone."

Lily sat back and pulled the blanket tight against the chill. It was good to learn something about her ancestors, to fill in the blanks a little. But it didn't begin to give her the answers she needed. What could these two tell her, even if they had the best intentions, even if they wanted to make her happy? She felt safe enough here, and there was a real chance she was moving closer to her goal while starting to find comfort in their unusual lifestyle. If Uncle Herman missed anyone, he had drawn that ache, along with all his other feelings, into the carapace of his odd personality. And Stepan seemed to care only about himself.

What about my father, my mother? She could not say the words. But neither could she sing with mindless joy, like the dumb storybook creatures, in the face of arbitrary, bewildering loss.

18

"What's this Russian flu, then?" Lily opened the *Britannica* on her lap. "I never heard of it until you mentioned it the other day."

"It's not as well-known as the Spanish version that hit the world in 1918 and killed millions of people," Stepan replied. "Have you heard of that one?" He tapped a small nail into the top of the window frame, stepped over the thin garland pooled on the floor, and drove in another nail two feet away.

"Well, um, no. Though wait, Grams mentioned one of her brothers got sick while fighting in World War I and died on the ship on the way home. Was that the flu, you think?" She looked up. "Do another nail between the windows, so it doesn't droop too much. What? I know how to do this. I've been doing it all my life."

He smiled. "All your life, huh? I'm surprised Herman agreed to let us decorate at all. First time since I've been living in this house." Stepan finished placing the nails and sat down. "Most likely it was the flu. Check your encyclopedia, but I'm pretty sure it killed more soldiers than the fighting did, the way it raced through the trenches and barracks and troop ships, with no effective remedy in sight."

"Huh. But the Russian one. Why Russian?" She flipped some pages. "It hardly says anything about it here, except that it happened and spread all over the world."

"That's where it started..."

"Oh, yeah. I see it." She read silently for a minute or so. "It says here even the royal families got sick, in Russia and Europe. Some even died."

"Put that down for a minute and come hold the end of this garland," Stepan said. "I have other work to do, you know."

"You do? A week before Christmas?"

Lily stood up, picked the garland up off the floor and cradled it, feeding it to Stepan a foot or so at a time. "So why is that? I mean, don't rich people have the best doctors? It's regular people who get sick in bunches and die, like in a plague or something. Right? Fix that loop in the middle there. Yeah, like that."

Stepan glanced at her but did as he was told, looping the garland evenly across both windows. "Yes. This disease was different because of the travel—all those luxury ships and railroads they were building that kept people in enclosed compartments for hours, days at a time. And no one likes to travel more than rich people do. So they got sick along with everybody else, with students and factory workers, who brought it home to their families. Any eggnog left from the other day?"

"Probably. You're the only one who likes it." Lily put the book back on the shelf. She followed him into the kitchen, rummaged in the refrigerator for the eggnog and took out an orange soda for herself. "I guess that's how Uncle Herman's grandparents got it, from being on the ship, and from his father the student coming back from Berlin, from the school and all. That's sad."

"Yes." Stepan emptied the carton into a glass and swirled in a bit of bourbon. "It's sad."

19

No one was home when Stepan came with the Christmas tree; no one was there to help him untie it from the roof of his car and drag it over the frozen snowless ground, past the bird feeders and into the house. Lily was at school. Uncle Herman had gone to the library for his monthly supply of reading material.

Uncle Herman read everywhere, except in the bathroom. He carried whichever book he was reading to the kitchen table, or his living room chair, or, in good weather, out to the tiny veranda he had added out back after he took possession of the house. More of a balcony, really, attached to his bedroom, railed all around with no steps to the ground. It was just big enough for one chair and a small square weather-beaten table, inviting no company.

The tree was a scant five feet tall and fit easily on top of an upturned crate in the corner of the living room. By the time Lily got home, Stepan had covered the crate with a lace-edged red cloth, set the tree in its stand, and strung it with multi-colored lights.

"Oh, hey," Lily said. "Cool beans. I asked Uncle Herman if we'd have a tree, but he only shrugged. Like I'm supposed to know what that means." She tossed her backpack on the couch. "I'm a good tree trimmer. Grams always let me help."

"Not until Christmas Eve," Stepan answered. When she started to ask why, he held up a hand. "Tradition."

"Yeah? What kind? From Hungary, I'll bet."

"Partly. When the Soviets were done messing with our holidays, things got a little mixed up." He leaned over the kitchen sink and scrubbed at the pine sap on his fingers with hot water and soap. "Want tea?"

She glanced at the empty coffee pot. "Yeah, okay."

While waiting for the water to boil, Stepan told her about Saint Nicholas, who brought presents in early December. "We call him Mikulas." He talked about the tree-trimming party, later, on Christmas Eve: family, friends, music, treats for children. "There were always treats, no matter how bleak the circumstances."

They took their cups into the living room.

"And my father was Ukrainian," Stepan said. "So, we also had *Ded Moroz*—Father Christmas." He wrapped one hand around his teacup. "One year—it may have been our first or second winter after leaving Hungary—my father said, 'Listen, I think I hear soft footsteps outside.' It was evening, we had just finished supper. I ran to the door and pulled it open. There, against the wall, was a small Christmas tree, and fresh tracks in the snow. Footsteps leading right up to our door."

"Wow," Lily breathed. "That's so sweet."

"I was thrilled, mystified. I believed, with the total faith of a child, that Father Christmas had brought me—*me*—a tree. That I was good." He set his cup down on its saucer with a sigh. "Or at least good enough. It didn't dawn on me until years later that my father set the whole thing up."

They heard Uncle Herman come in and drop a stack of books on the kitchen table.

"So how long did you keep the tree up, if you only trimmed it on Christmas Eve?" Lily asked, remembering how her grandmother, who started decorating right after Thanksgiving, had every crocheted trinket and elf figurine put away, the stripped tree at the curb by December 26th.

"My father was Orthodox, he observed Christmas on January

seventh. So we kept the tree up longer than most. Got to celebrate twice, you could say."

"How come?"

"It's a different calendar. Kind of complicated; you could look it up in your *Britannica*." He stood up, adjusted a row of lights, draping them deeper into the branches.

"You ever have candles?" Uncle Herman said from the doorway, his arms full of library books. His face was flushed right to the cuff of his wool cap. Lily couldn't tell if it was emotion, the effort of joining the conversation, or just his coming in from the cold. She tried not to look surprised at his unexpected question.

"On the tree?" Stepan went down on one knee, fixing the lights near the base to his satisfaction. "Yes. In Hungary. Tiny candles in star-shaped holders clipped to the ends of the branches. When it was time, my father would light them. We would stand, the grownups with their grog, we kids silenced by the beauty, the magic of it."

"I bet it was, I don't know, a little scary," Lily said. "I've only seen pictures, like in old books. Wasn't it dangerous?"

"Sure. That's why we stood and admired it before my father extinguished the candles and everyone sat down to dinner."

"Wow. Did you have candles, Uncle Herman, like, long ago?"

"Yeah, long ago." Uncle Herman bent his head to read the spines of the books he was holding. He selected *The Lusitania Disaster*, laid it on the end table next to his armchair, and made his way toward his room with the rest of the stack.

Stepan looked up, his glance attentive, sharp. "Why do you ask, Herman?" He grasped the arm of the couch and pulled himself up. "Was that what happened? The fire? Your parents, and those children? You never said."

"That was summer," Uncle Herman said, his hand on the

bedroom doorknob. "Started in the basement. They were sleeping." He pushed the door open. "I was in the Army."

"So why..." Lily hesitated, her lips pressed together. "...why don't you like to celebrate Christmas? Grams does, and she's your sister."

"What's to celebrate? Greedy merchants. People you barely know who pretend to care about you once a year. Stella can do what she wants." He went into his room and shut the door.

Lily stepped back from the undecorated tree. "Maybe he's right, you know? I mean, it's not about Baby Jesus or anything religious for us, not even for Grams." She sighed. "But I like it—the tree, the presents, the cards, even some of the lame songs. The cookies. Is that okay?"

"Of course it's okay. Nothing wrong with showing folks you remember them, if only once a year." Stepan picked up the empty teacups. "He grew up in a house full of people. It must be hard to remember the happy times and to deal with all those empty places at the table. You can't blame him for shutting down."

"Yeah." She took the cups from him and carried them into the kitchen.

20

A few days later, Lily called California for her grandmother's rum ball cookie recipe. "I can make little stars out of sugar cookies, and Uncle Herman gave me an old cookbook with some new kinds I can try. But there's nothing in there like your rum balls."

Stella chuckled. "When I was small, my mother made them with real rum. She kept the bottle from one year to the next, hidden on a high pantry shelf. My dad would poke his head into the kitchen every five minutes. 'Quality control,' he'd say. 'Just want to be sure you're using the best ingredients.' Mom had to give him a nip so he'd leave us alone to finish the baking."

Lily laughed. "Those cookies, they're the best."

"Yes. I found that recipe in the back of my mother's kitchen drawer, singed around the edges. I don't know how it escaped the fire. Everything else was destroyed or ruined. Everyone in the house died."

Lily bowed her head and listened to her grandmother's breathing. "Where were you?" *Why have we never talked about this?*

"I was staying with a friend, sneaking a secret date with my boyfriend."

"Grams—"

"She had beautiful handwriting, my mother. Elegant and fine, nothing like my scrawl. When I found the recipe, I sat right down on the floor in that charred house and cried."

"Oh, Grams. I'm so sorry. Did I make you feel bad? I'm sorry."

"It's not your fault, Lily. It was long, long ago. Herman was in the service. Everyone else was gone. When my fiancé decided to try writing for the movies, I came to California with him. There was no reason not to." Stella covered the mouthpiece and coughed, hard. "But it was many years before I could face making rum balls again. Many years."

Lily sat down. "I'm such a jerk. I didn't know those cookies made you sad. Grams, you should have told me!"

"We all have our sorrows, don't we. I loved making cookies with you. Why ruin the fun with sad stories? You had enough heartache of your own." She coughed again, softer now. "Well, enough of old times. I use rum extract, though. You know there's no liquor in my house."

"I know, Grams." *I looked*, she wanted to add, but didn't. "So, what do I need?"

"Oh, it's kind of complicated. I should send you the recipe."

Lily knew how hard that would be for her grandmother. She pictured Stella holding the writing pad with one hand while trying to still the shakes in the other long enough to write, the letters coming out large and loopy and uneven, the words crowded together or else wide apart, spikes alternating with squiggles that ran off the end of the page. "Just tell me. I can jot it down."

That done, Lily heard Stella sigh, the sound coming through the phone line in a quavery rush. "Are you happy, Lambkin?" Stella said.

Lily's breath caught in her throat. She was unprepared for the wave of feeling. Love and loss and guilt swirled in a dizzying eddy, the elements so intermingled it was impossible to tell them apart. "I guess so. Yeah, sure." What else could she say, how could she respond to the longing in the old woman's voice? "I miss you," is what came out.

And she realized it was true.

"Maybe we can have a visit in the summer," Stella suggested. "Oh, and the rum balls—they're best if you keep them in a tin for at least two weeks, especially if your uncle will let you use real rum."

"Oh, well, that's okay, either way. We can always have them after Christmas. Thanks, Grams." She added, "Love you," but the line had gone dead.

She stared at the phone. *Fuck*, she thought. *Why can't we all be happy, everybody at the same time?* You always had to choose one person over another, like it was some kind of rotation, some wheel of fortune game with winners and losers. As if you could even tell what winning felt like, how the good feeling slipped away, and you were left with nothing but doubt.

In her room, she lay down on the bed. *Is that what my father did? Spin the dial and take off? Only it landed on himself, on his own, what? Need, restlessness, fear.* Stepan's storybook childhood ruminations had left her with a sense of melancholy bordering on despair, a deep pull for what, exactly, she couldn't say. It's not as if she and Grams had failed to celebrate the holidays; there had always been joy and warmth, but not without a core of sadness that permeated both their lives. Alone with his memories all these years, did Uncle Herman really feel he had nothing to celebrate? Would Grams have felt that way if she hadn't had a child to love, first her own son and then herself, Lily, the unexpected resident in her home, her heart?

People had whole lives before you came along. They did things, took chances, made decisions. They laughed and worked and partied and cried. They hurt. When Lily was small, her grandmother was her whole universe; she took care of Lily's needs while shielding her from danger. *She put up with your stupid moods, your fresh mouth and bad behavior, idiot. Did you ever once wonder what her life might have been like without you?* What hopes had she set aside,

77

what paths chosen not to pursue because this child was thrust into her keeping? *Like there's nobody in the world but you.*

What did she, Lily, want—the thing she had left behind, or the one she'd never had? Maybe, to echo Stepan's words, she hadn't been good enough to deserve a place in her father's life. Maybe he had sensed a defect in her that gave him license to leave. *Bullshit,* she thought. *How good does a baby have to be? All I did wrong was get born.*

She reached at random for a tape among the ones scattered on the shelf next to Uncle Herman's restored cassette player, the tremor in her grandmother's voice still clear in her head. "As if you don't know what it's like to run away, Lily," she said out loud. "You're not so different."

She turned up the volume and lay back, letting Janis Joplin shriek into her ears. Ecstasy laced with pain, just the thing.

21

On the afternoon of the twenty-fourth, Stepan and Lily trimmed the tree. "Come and help, Uncle Herman," she said. "Have some fun."

He snapped his book shut. "Car needs an oil change."

"Right now? There's a snowstorm coming," Stepan objected.

"That's why."

Lily glanced at her great-uncle, then at Stepan, who was sorting through a box of ornaments. She lifted a glass bird to the light and blew some dust off the rainbow tail feathers. "This one of yours, Uncle Herman? It looks old-fashioned. Pretty." She clipped the bird to a branch nearest the window, to give it a view of a world it would never know.

"No. None of them," the old man muttered. He put on his wool cap and work boots and went out.

Lily let out a breath. "Why's he have to be like that?" She teared up and turned her head aside so Stepan wouldn't see.

He hung a filigreed ball and reached for a gilded pinecone. "The ornaments are mine. My mother collected them, adding two or three every year. We had a custom among our friends. When we visited each other during the holidays, we would take an ornament from their tree and hang it on ours, and they would do the same."

"What if they took, like, the best one?"

"That was a chance you took. We enjoyed seeing our ornaments make the rounds, spreading goodwill and friendship. I don't know how it started, but in the end, we lost track of who owned which trinket." He handed her a small gray rabbit, the paint chipped off its ears, exposing the wood underneath. "But this one was my favorite. I admit I cried when our neighbor claimed it and took it home. My mother tried to comfort me, but my father said, 'Don't get so attached. There's more than one rabbit in the world to love.' Took me years to figure out what that meant."

"You mean, like, women? That's cold, especially to say to a little kid. How did your mother feel about that?"

"She laughed, I think. I was, as you say, a little kid."

Lily shook her head. "Grownups are weird. How'd you get it back? The rabbit?"

"I don't remember. Maybe my mother had something to do with it." He sighed. "Put it down here near the bottom. Rabbits like to hide."

Lily hung the rabbit deep in the lower branches of the tree. She sat down and shook her head again.

"What?" Stepan closed the box.

"It's crazy how stuff that happens when you're a kid follows you all your life. Like, nobody gets it right, you know?"

On Christmas day they opened gifts around noon, Lily in mismatched socks, and a sweater over her nightshirt.

"Did you make this?" Stepan unwound a long yellow scarf out of a cylindrical oatmeal carton trimmed with silver foil stars. He looked regal in a silky wine-colored dressing gown and leather slippers.

Lily nodded. "You'd probably like brown or green better, but that was too boring. I figured you could use a touch of color. And yellow was on sale, cheap."

Stepan wrapped the scarf twice around his neck and swiveled his body from side to side for inspection. "Thanks, kid. It's my favorite color, after brown and green."

"It is not," she laughed. "Anyway. The starting end's a little ragged, but I'd have to rip the whole thing out to fix it. Oh." She snapped her fingers. "I could put fringe on it, to hide it, if you want. It can't be that hard."

"Leave it alone," Uncle Herman put in. "It looks fine."

Stepan just smiled.

"Wait till you see yours," Lily made a half-embarrassed face.

Uncle Herman unwrapped his lumpy parcel. A circular knitting needle with four or five inches of scarf on it lay in his lap. A ball of yellow yarn rolled off and came to rest under his chair. "What..."

"Okay. Here's what happened. I wanted to make mittens, but I messed up the thumb. Came out kinda gross, if you really want to know. Looked like—well, never mind." She covered her mouth with both hands and giggled. "So I started a scarf instead. It's not finished."

"I see."

"Besides, mittens are so kindergarten. It was a dumb idea."

"Not dumb," Uncle Herman said. His eyes crinkled just short of a smile. "Warmer than gloves. I guess you want this back."

Lily took the bundle from him. "I'll get it done before school starts next month. Promise."

"Don't promise," the old man said.

"Why not? I really mean it."

"Exactly." He looked away, ran his hands down his twill work pants.

What's that about? Nora? Or other people who promised to return and then went and died instead. The thought flashed through her mind and receded. This was not the time to ask for explanations.

Uncle Herman reached into the pocket of his flannel shirt and handed her an envelope. A bank envelope, the kind tellers

81

stuff your money into when you cash your paycheck, First Federal Credit Union printed in blue letters on one side. Lily lifted the flap and peeked inside. "Wow. Fifty. Thanks."

"Buy some clothes," Uncle Herman said. "You look like a bum."

Stepan knelt in front of the tree and slid a large package in reindeer wrap toward Lily's chair. "You're one to talk, Herman. When's the last time you bought new pants? 1960? Be nice." He pulled himself up, groaning with the effort. "Open it, Lily. It's for you."

She tore into the paper like a three-year-old. The men watched her peel long strips of paper off the box, crumple them into balls and toss them in a heap on the floor. "A boom box," she said when the object emerged from its wrapping. "Hey. Thanks."

"For your tapes," Stepan clarified. "It has a radio, too. Here." He reached into the pocket of his robe. "Extra batteries."

"What's wrong with the player she's got?" Uncle Herman demanded.

"It's old. It could jam up and ruin her tapes. And this one's portable. She can take it out in the yard."

"What the hell for?"

"Stop it," Lily said from the doorway. She had escaped to the kitchen when the argument started. "I like it, but I'll keep using the old one for now, okay? Have some fruit punch and cookies. I made them myself." She set the tray down on the coffee table.

The room filled with the sound of crunching. When Stepan went to retrieve the Jim Beam to spike his drink, Uncle Herman scowled but ignored him. "Call your grandmother," he said to Lily.

Stella's voice sounded faint, unsteady, but seemed to strengthen as she and Lily talked. When Lily described her knitting misadventures, Stella chuckled. "You never did things the easy way."

Lily listened for rancor, alert to any hint of implied criticism, but found none. "Yeah," she agreed. "I guess so. Are you having dinner with Margrit?"

"Margrit? She may live next door, but since she found herself a boyfriend, we never talk. Can you believe it? A boyfriend, at our age. I see them walking sometimes, arm in arm, holding each other up."

Lily couldn't be sure there wasn't a trace of envy in her grandmother's words. "C'mon, Grams. You're not that old." But she was, and Lily knew it. She felt a rush of guilt for having run out, leaving Stella alone. "What's for dinner?"

"Oh, no dinner. There's a Christmas lunch at the senior center, I'll go there. They send a van to pick us up and bring us home; they even give us a turkey sandwich and a slice of fruitcake for later. What are you cooking?"

"Meatloaf. Did you know it's Uncle Herman's favorite food? After corned beef hash from a can." Lily glanced at her great-uncle for a reaction. Deep in his chair, his feet an inch or two off the floor, he was engrossed in his book and gave no indication of having heard her remark. Stepan dozed on the couch, mouth open, the scarf bunched in his lap, his head pillowed on the backrest. *Like a big baby,* Lily thought. *A big baby with gray roots and a drinking habit.*

"Meatloaf?" Stella echoed.

"Yeah. But I make it good, with hard-boiled eggs inside, and mushroom sauce. I wish you could eat with us," Lily burst out. She suddenly missed the old woman, her fussiness, her warmth, her papery veined hands. Her smile. She pictured the room, the telephone centered on a doily on the dark wood table—was it mahogany?—next to the pink-and-green striped sofa. She saw the lacy curtains and the chronicle of her own life, from babyhood through memorable moments and school portraits, in a gallery of photographs on the wall. *Who would miss me if I disappeared? What am I doing here?*

As if remembering her mission, she asked, "Anything from my father?"

"No," Stella sighed. "Nothing for months now, for me or for you. Not even a Christmas card. I hope he's okay."

"Mmm. You take care, Grams. Don't stay out late."

22

Lily didn't buy any clothes. She put the fifty, still in its bank envelope, into the postcard box. For once, she didn't look at the cards before closing the lid. She knew what they said.

If you don't want to be part of my life, why can't you leave me alone, DAD? Do you even exist, or is this some colossal put-on?

The next week brought a letter from her grandmother.

> Look at this! Margrit and her boyfriend gave me a typewriter. A word processor, they called it. It's not too heavy, and very quiet, not like the old Olympia I used at work. And if I make a mistake, I can erase it, just like that. Isn't that wonderful? I make a lot of mistakes. Now I can write to you and send you recipes. A good cook always needs new ideas, right? Please write back and tell me how you're doing. Tell me about school. Send me some news about your uncle. We're close in age, so he must have his aches and pains, like me, but you know he doesn't like to talk much. Thank you for the Christmas call, it was good to hear your voice. Long-distance calls are expensive, though, so write to me, won't you?

The letter was signed, "Love, Grams" in pencil, the lines going from thick with pressure to barely there at the end.

And there was, in a separate, smaller envelope, a postcard. In the foreground, a large fountain, surrounded by four smaller ones. Behind them, people strolled along a wide avenue or sat on benches under a line of trees. Beyond that, an impossibly blue sea. The message read:

> Nietzsche, Friedrich Wilhelm, 1844-1900. German philosopher. The son of a minister, he was appointed to the chair of classical philology at Basel in 1869. Nervous disturbances and eye trouble forced him to leave Basel; he moved from place to place in a vain effort to improve his health until 1889, when he became hopelessly insane. In his work, he looked to the superman who would represent the highest passion and creativity and would live at a level beyond the conventional standards of good and evil.

> Yours truly

Along the upper edge, in printed letters, he had inked, ABLE TO LEAP TALL BUILDINGS, and added little whorls resembling whirlpools. As always, there was no greeting, no signature, only the usual *Columbia Encyclopedia* attribution.

"It's Theodosia, in Crimea, USSR," Stepan said when she asked him about the Russian words on the back. "1991." He lowered the magnifying glass he'd used to decipher the tiny print nearly obliterated by the compact written text that spilled over into the address box. "Look, it even has pre-stamped five-kopek postage." He paused to read the message, raised an eyebrow, but said nothing about it.

Lily took the card into her room. What was her father trying to say? Was this another strange attempt to further her education or only a sick joke? Was there a cry for help in the references to poor health, insanity, good and evil? If so, what was she supposed to do about it? She stared at the picture, at the inviting scenery meant to entice vacationers or serve as a memento of good times past. Where did he get a card from the Soviet Union, anyway? The thought that he might be a spy gave her a little thrill, but she dismissed it as a romantic fantasy. She didn't know where he was, but surely someone did. Someone maybe as close as West Point.

23

Lily was at the kitchen table drawing a map of South America when Stepan came in from a two-day sales trip.

"You're up late." He slid his overnight bag away from the door and draped his jacket on top. "School project?"

"It's Friday," she mumbled without looking up. "I can stay up if I like." Lily sketched in part of the coastline, following a full-page illustration in the *Britannica*. "Gotta get this outline done before I fill in the countries."

Stepan poured himself a drink and sat down. "Can't you just trace it? That's what I always did. It's easier."

"I don't need it easier, I need it bigger. Anyway, it's fun. A kid in my class showed me how to enlarge the grid, then fill it in square by square, by hand. His father's the drafting teacher, so he knows what he's talking about." She held up the poster board. "Looks pretty good, see?"

"Huh. Clever. I never would have thought of that." He stirred the ice in his glass with a finger. "When's it due?"

"Monday. I already wrote the report, just need to finish this map." Lily put the poster down and kept drawing. "There's ham if you want a sandwich."

"No thanks, I ate." He drained the glass, refilled it, added a splash of seltzer. "Imagine being an explorer, or an early cartographer, filling the details in as you go. By hand."

"Mm. Cool." She finished the narrow tip of the continent and started up the east coast. "You can hang around if you want, just don't move the table." She glanced up, sharply. "Or spill anything."

Stepan got up, stood at the counter with his back to the sink. "Listen. I wanted to talk to you." He hesitated, cleared his throat. "I have an idea."

"Yeah? What kind?"

"I'm going to see a couple of bookstores next week, Wednesday, near West Point."

"Yeah, so?"

"You could ride along."

Lily stopped drawing. She looked up. Stepan swirled the contents of his half-empty glass, smiling. "How many of those you have today? I'm in school Wednesday."

"You could skip half a day—"

"No, Stepan, I couldn't." She took an angry breath, let it out. "Besides, it's no good."

"What's no good? The map? Looks—"

"Going to West Point. It's no good. I called them."

"You did? When?" His voice sounded higher, louder. He put the glass in the sink. "Does Herman know?"

Lily pushed her chair back, started to gather her things. "I don't need Uncle Herman's permission to use the phone."

"Well, who did you talk to? What did they say?"

"Well, nothing." She struck a pose. "'The US Army has no locator services for military personnel.'"

"Who told you this?"

She waved her hands in the air. "Some lady. They bounced my call around for half an hour. She's the only one who would talk to me."

"Lily, what did she say, exactly?"

"She threw the alphabet at me." Lily read from her notebook: "DMDC. Defense Manpower Data Center for military verification of service. Name. DOB. SS number." She lowered the notebook. "But they won't tell me where he is. Wash that glass."

"Yes, okay. Okay. What else did you learn? There must be something you can do."

"Sure. I can..." she read, "...submit a request for contact which will be forwarded to the service member, who may respond if interested.'"

"Well, that's helpful, right?"

"Hell, no! Don't you get it? He knows where I am, how to reach me."

Stepan washed the glass, dried it, put it away. "There's nothing—"

"I can contact the Red Cross, if it's an emergency. But they still won't tell me where he is. And it's not an emergency."

They fell silent. Lily closed the *Britannica,* stacked her school things, gathered her pencils.

Stepan sighed. "Maybe we should still go. Maybe they'll tell me."

She shook her head. "You're not family, and I'm not eighteen. They'll only tell you if you're a veteran looking for a buddy from your unit." Her hands dropped to her sides, her shoulders slumped. "So that's that. You win, Dad. You win."

24

In January, Lily turned fifteen. The celebration brunch was a cooperative affair: Lily made crepes, served, as her Grams had taught her, European style, with sour cream and jam, oranges and bananas laced with honey on the side. Uncle Herman contributed coffee and perfectly fried eggs, his specialty. Stepan surprised everyone with a dozen pink carnations in an earthenware crock.

"Hey, cool." Lily rotated the crock to examine it from all sides, running her fingers over its bumps and ridges. "It's handmade, right? I can use it for utensils or something."

"Your sleeve's in the sour cream," Uncle Herman said, while Stepan beamed.

The day passed like an ordinary Sunday. Stepan dozed through an old movie on TV. Uncle Herman read a book, getting up now and then to refill his coffee mug and check on the suet feeders he'd added to see the birds through the winter. Lily stayed in her room, napping, alternating between the Beach Boys and the Stones on her cassette player.

Toward evening, she made her way to the kitchen. The men could hear her rummaging in the refrigerator, pushing stuff around in the cabinets. "How's spaghetti?" she called out. "With the snowstorm and all, we didn't go shopping."

Stepan got up, stretched, and yawned. "Tell you what," he said. "Let's go out. My treat. What do you want?"

"Ice cream," Lily replied without hesitation. She stood in the kitchen doorway, her hair spiked on one side and flat on the other, hands tucked into her sweatshirt's kangaroo pocket. "Not from a box." She glanced at her uncle before he could say, 'Look in the freezer.' "The real kind, from an ice cream place. Only they're all closed, being winter."

"Not all. I know one in PA, a dairy farm. I always stop there when I'm in the area. They serve hamburgers and have their own creamery."

"PA? There's snow on the ground. Two feet," Uncle Herman snorted.

"On the ground, not on the road. It's maybe twenty-five miles from here. We can be there in half an hour or so."

"You two go. I've got pork and beans."

"Don't be an ass, Herman. It's her birthday."

Lily had left the room but soon reappeared, wearing her parka, pulling a knit cap over her ears. She bent to get her snow boots from the mat near the back door and sat down to lace them up. "I want you to come, Uncle Herman." She raised her head. They locked eyes, her determined expression meeting his obstinate one. "Please."

She sat in the back, feet planted on the hump between the seats, her chin on her knees. "I brought a tape," she said, once they had navigated the winding local roads and were on the highway. "The Eurythmics. Everybody likes the Eurythmics." She thrust her arm between the front seats.

Uncle Herman took the cassette. He turned it over in his hands as if examining an unfamiliar and potentially dangerous object. "Pop it in," Stepan urged. "This Beamer's a '98, plays tapes and CDs, both."

They drove in silence while Annie Lennox sang about sweet dreams and the universal quest for happiness, or at least satisfaction.

Lily bobbed along, mouthing the words; even Stepan tapped the beat out on the steering wheel with one finger. Uncle Herman kept his eyes on the road, hands on thighs, shoulders tense.

"So this place has hamburgers AND ice cream? From the same cows?" Lily asked when the song ended. "I mean, after they stop giving milk, they get to be dinner?"

"No." Stepan's mouth twitched at the corners, but he did not laugh. "Hamburger comes from beef cattle, not dairy cows."

"Good. 'Cause that would be like, heartless. Thanks for all the cheese and cream, now off you go, 'bye. What happens to old cows, anyway?"

"Dog food," Uncle Herman deadpanned.

Stepan slapped the steering wheel but said nothing. Lily sat back in her seat, deflated. "Play the tape again, okay?" she said in a small voice.

The restaurant was in an old white two-story farmhouse, with a railed wrap-around porch and sky-blue trim. A carved Jersey the size of a Great Dane flanked the painted double doors, its tan back worn smooth behind the shoulder blades from countless bareback photo ops. Above the cow hung a slotted board with the day's ice cream flavors: vanilla, Dutch chocolate, butter pecan, pumpkin pie, blackberry swirl.

"I love it already." Lily stroked the cow's broad head. "What a great idea, Stepan."

Uncle Herman held the door open. "Who am I to disagree."

They feasted on thick hamburgers topped with garlic cheese, ordered extra helpings of hand-cut fries and German coleslaw. "This is good," Uncle Herman admitted with a fleeting smile. "Better than pork and beans."

The ice cream had to be double scoops—no one could decide

on only one flavor. "Dutch chocolate and pumpkin pie," Stepan announced as if he'd been thinking about it all day. "You, Herman?"

"Vanilla and butter pecan."

"Hit me with Dutch chocolate and blackberry swirl," Lily decided. "In a waffle cone."

They gorged themselves in companionable silence. There were no words.

On the way home, Uncle Herman took the back seat and soon fell asleep, first sitting up, then giving in to the primal urge to nap after sated hunger, curled on the seat, one arm over his face.

Lily sighed. "That was like, divine, Stepan. Best birthday ever."

"Yeah. I go out of my way to stop there when I'm on the road. Glad you liked it."

Lily moved her feet to make room for the bag of extra pints to take home. "I love the cow pictures on the walls, how each one has its name on it. Like they're celebrities or something. Family. And the babies—those calves are too adorable. Too bad they don't get to stay with their mothers."

She grew quiet. Stepan glanced at her. He sped up to pass a convoy of trucks, then settled into cruising speed. They drove by wooded stretches, bare-limbed trees silhouetted against a violet sky, only the evergreens still laden with snow. Here and there, small gatherings of deer nosed in the drifts at the road's edge in search of last year's grass.

Lily sat with a hand over her mouth, leaning forward a little.

"Nice landscape," Stepan said. "New York winter." When Lily didn't reply, he ventured,

"What's on your mind?"

"Nothing." Lily looked at him as if to appraise the seriousness of the question. "Same old stuff." She turned to stare out her side window. "Did you know that when a calf is born, they leave it with the cow only until she starts making milk? Then they take the calf away before the mother and baby can bond, or know each other." She paused. "I read that in Uncle Herman's *Farm Life* magazine."

"Yes," Stepan said, noncommittal.

"So, like those calves, I don't have a mother. No memory, no pictures, no history, no bond. Nothing. Just a shoe box of old music cassettes. But I've got Grams, and she's like, the best person on earth. So I'm not even curious anymore."

"Okay, but—"

"But the father. Why won't he leave me alone? No, I don't mean that. I kind of like the stupid cards, the game. Trying to figure out what he's getting at, and all. But still."

"Maybe they don't mean anything. You'd have to get into his skin to know what he's thinking. Walk in his shoes. Maybe he just wants you to know he hasn't forgotten you.'

"Could be. Or maybe he's like, nuts, in his own special way. That would be okay too. I mean, you and Uncle Herman are kinda odd, but you're still good people." Lily shifted around to face him. "But sometimes I want to scream. Like, You, father, who are you? What do you want from me? What's the fucking punchline?" Her voice was low, agitated, with a tremor bordering on tears.

They listened to Uncle Herman's rhythmic wheezing. When he let out a long, slow fart, they cracked their windows open and laughed.

Stepan guided the car onto the country road toward home. The snow shone blue in the car's high beams. "You ever think to write back?"

26

Lily let her gaze drift from the assigned reading. The Labor Movement. Frances Perkins, the first woman to hold a cabinet post, who witnessed the Triangle factory fire and championed laws against child labor, gave us minimum wage and the forty-hour work week. With Frances in his ear and Eleanor at his elbow, FDR had no choice but to do the right thing. "See? Women get stuff done," Lily said.

She thought about that folk singer classroom guest, whose name she had forgotten, but whose casual stance and bony intensity remained imprinted on her mind: pale denim shirt, black jeans, work boots, one foot up on the seat of a chair, her banged-up guitar on her knee. Nothing smooth about her.

"Kids like you," the singer said, her low voice hoarse like she'd run it through a grater. "Why aren't you working in a cotton mill or on a factory assembly line? 'Cause people stood up, or lay down and died, some of them, so you could grow up, go to school, get a decent wage when you got a job."

She sang about young girls locked in a burning factory, falling to their death, clothes aflame, onto the sidewalk many stories below. How crowds of people came to their funeral, marched in the streets. *You can't scare me, I'm stickin' to the union,* Lily sang to herself, knowing the words came from another protest song. Not caring.

Her glance caught Uncle Herman's coffee mug and bowl on the kitchen drainboard, the chili can on top of the trash bag at the door. He always cleaned up, never left dishes or messes for someone else to deal with later. As if he skimmed over life, leaving the barest ripple on the surface, scant evidence of having been here at all.

He was in the other room, his presence marked by the whisper of turning pages, the occasional muted cough. Now and then, she heard him make his way to the bathroom, leaving the door open while he checked the feeders. The chair she'd offered for his birdwatching had been moved aside, rejected, and now held a few of Stepan's magazines—*The Atlantic, Publisher's Weekly*. Uncle Herman preferred to stand, making it clear she wasn't the only one who didn't like being told what to do.

She thought back to her birthday dinner, reliving the glow of good food, an enjoyable time with her unlikely companions. *Killer ice cream*, she remembered, and smiled. Then Stepan's words about writing back, finding a way to complete the circle, or at least make contact. Get some answers.

Had she ever thought about it? Not really. Her father's correspondence didn't invite a reply. In all the years he'd written to her, he had never asked a single question—about her life, her plans, her health, her troubles. Not even stupid getting-to-know-you stuff, like her favorite color or candy bar. So what could she possibly say? *Thanks for trying, but what the hell do you think you're doing to my life? Or, hey, this is cool. Keep the cards coming. Maybe one day I'll understand what the point is. I'll be enlightened; the truth will be revealed and everything will be forgiven.*

Because isn't that what you want? To be forgiven for following my mother's example and passing me off to another pair of hands? Lucky for me those hands had a heart attached to them, and I guess you knew that. So, yeah, thanks for that, anyway. You could have done worse, left me on the mayor's doorstep, or wherever unwanted babies end up these days.

My mother did the right thing, I suppose, in her own dopey way. Why start wrecking this baby's life when she wasn't yet done screwing up her own? And you were what, thirty, when she was sixteen? The responsible adult male with a taste for chicks raised by the Woodstock generation.

Sixty-nine. That's when my mother was born, wasn't it, right after all the naked mud dancing, the good times to end all good times. I picture her groovin' to that California lifestyle while boycotting grapes, picketing chemical plants and restaurants known for abusive worker treatment. Places where she'd never held a job and never would, I'll bet, her actions coming from some vague sense of justice she'd picked up from listening to Joan Baez. Peace, man.

Maybe she's okay. Maybe she earned enough dough selling macramé hangings to beachfront craft shops to keep her in cheap wine and day-old bread from the supermarket bargain rack. Or maybe she went vegan, opened a pint-sized juice bar, dealing pot on the side, serving her time when she got caught. Maybe she's dead. Or homeless, sleeping on the beach, no longer bothering to cover her tracks.

When I was small, I used to imagine she was nearby, that she watched me and Grams do our shopping, go to the park, walk to school. Well, that only happens in sappy novels and TV movies, where everything turns out for the best, with tearful confessions and lots of hugging. Real people can't live like that—it's like believing the dead see everything you do, that they watch you when you think you're alone and shake their heads at your foolishness. That idea's enough to make you bonkers.

So I lied. I do wonder about her, how maybe she remembers I exist, sometimes. But I don't wonder enough to find out or to make myself sick over it.

But you, Dad. What's your excuse? You think you're the first

101

guy on earth who was unprepared for parenthood? Ready or not, you made me. Here I am. Either find the courage to step out of whatever dark hole you're hiding in, show your face, call me by my name—or leave me alone.

How do you say that, any of it?

"You start," Lily said to the empty kitchen. She ripped a page out of her history notebook and wrote, in small careful script across the top:

My name is LILY.

She stared at the words awhile, then folded the paper into quarters, stuffed it into an envelope with yellowed edges she found in a junk drawer, and wrote the APO address on the outside. She added her return address—her name and Uncle Herman's, just to be sure. She sealed the envelope and left it on the counter for Uncle Herman or Stepan to mail. She didn't have a stamp.

27

The card was oversized, longer and wider than any of the others by at least an inch all around. It showed a Siberian gray squirrel, sepia-toned like a vintage illustration, posed high in an ancient tree, each claw and whisker etched with precision. A handsome specimen, with a white belly and feathery tail, it offered the viewer its profile with as much dignity a rodent could muster.

> Monasticism: form of religious life, usually conducted in a community under a common rule...Monasticism is traditionally of two kinds: the more usual form is known as the *cenobic*, and is characterized by a completely communal style of life; the second, the *eremitic*, entails a hermit's life of almost unbroken solitude...The term *contemplative* is ordinarily applied to the life of monks and nuns who are enclosed, i.e., who rarely leave the monastery or convent in which they live and work. [Excerpted from longer entry.]
>
> Yours truly.

Again, no greeting, no signature. Just the *Columbia Encyclopedia* attribution.

Lily lay on her bed and stared at the card. Had he gone completely around the bend? It had taken two months exactly, to the day, for the new missive to arrive. The postmark was APO Europe. So he was gone again. There was no need to go to West Point. What would they tell her, a kid, anyway? She had read how they put you on a bus and give you a tour, pointing out buildings, training areas, sports fields, monuments, landmarks. Big deal. It wasn't cheap, either. Why spend money she didn't have? She already knew no one would be willing to answer her questions.

But there, on the card, above Uncle Herman's street address, there was her name. And above his unit and APO designation, there was his. Lily and Mark finally linked by the same last name for the whole world to see. Acknowledgment. Tenuous, perhaps halfhearted or even grudging, but acknowledgment just the same.

Halfhearted? "No," she said. "I don't believe that." Lily had always felt, since the first card—the snowman, her favorite—a sense of good intention. If the card selection seemed random, maybe he was using whatever came to hand. And the puzzling messages seemed haphazard, as if he opened the *Columbia Encyclopedia* with his eyes closed and used the first entry his finger landed on. But underneath it all she felt a sly humor, an undercurrent of affection. Just because he knew nothing about being a father didn't mean he didn't care. Did it?

She spent some time pondering the monastic message. It might have something to do with his frame of mind; maybe he was feeling isolated, assigned to duty in some virtual Siberia. Maybe he *was* in Siberia, along with the squirrel and whatever else lived there. What was it like? She would look it up in the *Britannica*. "Huh," she said. "Aren't we a pair, Dad, with our encyclopedias."

Lily ran a finger along the contours of the card, noting its worn edges, the slight discoloration of its once-white surface, the tiny smudge in the upper right-hand corner. She looked again, closer. The smudge ended in a curved line, fine as an eyelash.

She slid off the bed, took the card to the window to catch the last of the late-winter light. She held it up to her face, then moved it back, crossing her eyes to examine the tiny sketch. "Holy fuck," she said. "It can't be."

In Uncle Herman's room, next to the book on his bedside table, she found a magnifying glass, retreated to the kitchen and turned on the light. She moved the glass up and down until the smudge came into focus. She stared at it as if it might shift or disappear. Put the magnifying glass down. Went back to her room for the other cards and spread them out on the kitchen table.

It was there on every one, in the corner next to the postmark, or somewhere along the bottom edge, or concealed among the drawings of plants and animals that adorned the text. How had she missed it all these years?

Uncle Herman came in from outside and stamped his feet on the doormat before taking off his boots. "More snow," he said. "And ice." Stepan was right behind him.

"It's a lily," she said. "A goddam lily." She held up the squirrel card. "Look. No, there, in the corner."

Stepan set his sample case down. He brushed the snow off his shoulders, took off his gloves, slapped the leather palms together before slipping the gloves, neatly folded, into his coat pockets. He examined the card. "It sure is." He gestured at the others scattered on the table. "On all of them?"

"All of them! I'm such a dumbass. I never saw it before."

Uncle Herman reached into the oatmeal cylinder that served as a cookie jar. "How's that make you dumb if you can't see what somebody's trying to hide?"

"There was this book I had when I was little." Lily picked the cards up one by one and stacked them together. "It had a tiny kitten on every page—peeking out of a basket, or squeezed between books on the shelf, behind the pillow, or in the flowerpot. I loved that book." She watched Stepan peel off his galoshes and line them up on the mat. "You're the only person in the world who wears those."

"They keep the shoes clean and the feet dry. What happened to the kitten in the story?"

"That's the best part. The story wasn't about the kitten. It was probably about sharing or going to bed or being nice to the new baby. Who remembers? I cared only about the kitten. Finding it made me feel clever, and it made me laugh, even after I had memorized every page." She laid the cards into their tin.

Stepan looked puzzled. "And you think your father knew this book?"

"I doubt it. Maybe. I don't know! That's not the point!" She slammed the tin shut.

Uncle Herman took another cookie. "Need more of these," he said, brushing the crumbs off his chin. He shuffled through the mail, leaving Stepan's catalogs and letters on the table.

"The point is he was addressing you on every card and you didn't know it." Stepan draped his coat on its wooden hanger and exchanged his shoes for slippers.

"Yes! Like he's been saying, This is for you. Did you find it? Isn't this fun?" Lily made a wry face. "And I'm like, What are you telling me? What's the story? See? Like a whiny dumbass."

"People shouldn't play games," Uncle Herman said. He tossed the junk mail in the trash and headed for his room, bills in hand. "What's for dinner?"

28

It wasn't Stella who answered the phone when Lily called to wish her a happy birthday. "Margrit? Where's Grams? Can I talk to her?"

"Oh, Lily, she is not here. I just come to get her slippers. You know, in the hospital they give you only the paper ones."

"Hospital?"

"She falls down and breaks her arm, last evening. And now they say she has the pneumonia, too. So she must stay. I was going to call you, in a minute." Margrit sounded flustered, but also a bit self-important. Useful.

"Wait. What?"

"Your grandma. She breaks her arm," Margrit paused. "You know, here, by the hand." Lily could almost see her raise her arm to demonstrate.

"Wrist? You mean wrist? She broke her wrist?"

"Yes. Yes, wrist. Thank you."

"When? How?"

"Last evening. We are having coffee and cake, talking, talking. Oof." She let out a big sigh. "My language. I am forgetting the words."

"It's okay, Margrit. I get you. Just tell me what happened."

"So. We are talking about babies. Is funny, yes? Two old ladies talking about babies. Your grandma says, 'My boy Mark, he was so fat, like little Buddha. Here, I show you.' And she goes to get the album, but it is too high, so she stands on a chair and I say, no, no, don't do that. And then she falls down."

Margrit stopped talking. Lily could hear her breathing as if she'd been hiking uphill on a hot day. "Okay, okay, relax. It's good you were there."

"The top of the cabinet, for dishes. It is too high. Who keeps pictures so high? Your grandma, sometimes she is not so smart."

Lily let this pass. "So then you took her to the hospital?"

"I call the 911. The ambulance takes her, and I come after. And I wait, one, two hours. They make, you know, the x-ray, then put the bandage around."

Lily imagined Margrit making circles in the air, wrapping the unseen limb. She smiled in spite of herself, recovered and asked, "So then, you said, pneumonia?"

"Yes. She is coughing, coughing. A long time now, you know. Many months. So they make the new x-ray and the doctor says, you stay here, Madam. You are too sick for home."

"Wow." Lily passed her free hand over her hair, the spikes tickling her palm. "Is she okay? What time'd you get home?"

"Two o'clock, maybe. Then I sleep, but not so good. She was resting. Now I go again, bringing her slippers and some magazines. Thank you for calling, Lily."

"Thank me? I just wanted to say happy birthday. You saved her life."

She hung up and sat very still, the hospital information note quivering in her hand. Why hadn't she noticed her grandmother coughing, a long time now? "Grams," she said. "I'm so sorry."

She had not moved when Uncle Herman came home, an hour or so later. The late afternoon light, diffused through gathering spring clouds, lay in the corners of the living room like a theater scrim, blurring the outlines of the furniture, the unlit lamp, the telephone. She heard him outside, pouring birdseed from its twenty-pound bag into the mouse-proof galvanized trash can he kept near the back door.

Lily had asked him once, months ago when they were first learning to know each other, "How come you're so crazy for birds?" He'd been standing at his usual post, in the bathroom, hands clasped behind his back. "I mean, I get it how they're pretty, and sing, and are like, free and all. But you're—" She struggled to find the word, decided against 'obsessed' and 'fanatical,' and let the phrase hang unfinished.

"Not so free," he replied after a pause. "Always looking for food, hiding from hawks and cats. On the move. Singing is for marking turf, for mating. For danger. Not for our pleasure." He spoke without turning to face her, his eyes fixed on the flurry of activity outside.

"Huh. I guess I knew that. But still."

"Look at them. Different colors, sizes, beaks, tails. But they know their own, stick together. Even though they're all birds." He looked at her then. It was a passing glance, but she thought she'd seen sadness in it, and anger, too, and something else she couldn't name. Yearning, regret?

Remembering it now, she realized it had been the longest conversation they'd ever had. And one of the most revealing. *They know their own, even though they're all birds.*

She forced herself off the couch and came out to meet him, holding the note out like a proclamation. "Here," she said. "It's Grams. She's sick." She laid the paper down on the table and fled to her room. He wasn't going to see her cry.

29

Lily sat on her bed until the only thing she could see were the hands of her alarm clock, glowing their message into the windowless room. Eight-fifteen. She thought she smelled something cooking. Potatoes, maybe.

She had stopped crying long ago but felt unable to move, a damp lump of paper tissue clutched in her fist.

Someone knocked. "Yeah," she said.

Uncle Herman opened the door. "Come eat."

With the light behind him, Lily couldn't see his face, but the slope of his shoulders and the way his arms hung down told her he wasn't feeling so great, either. "Did you call the hospital? What did Grams say?"

"She wasn't in her room. It was afternoon there. They do procedures, tests. Come on."

Lily didn't move.

Uncle Herman came in and turned on the bedside lamp. Lily looked up at him, then glanced at Stepan, whose frame now filled the doorway. She lowered her eyes. When she noticed her fingers reflexively squeezing the wet tissue, she tossed it aside and pressed her hands between her knees.

"I came here to find somebody who doesn't want to be found." She spoke in a soft monotone, her eyes glassy. "And I ran away from somebody who really needs me. Loves me." She shook her head slowly. "That's the word, isn't it. The word I never hear, not in this house, not from my father and his dopey cards, not from anybody.

Only Grams.

"I thought I was tough and smart. I could do anything I wanted, look after myself, go my own way. I'm not tough. My heart feels like a marshmallow, my brain is a beehive with no one in charge, all buzzing and nothing gets done. So I'm not smart either."

"Look—" Uncle Herman started to say, but she held up a hand to stop him.

"I have to go. I can't let Grams suffer alone. I have to help her, like she helped me. Did anybody ask her if she wanted a little kid to raise? But she did it, while I..." Lily teared up, reached for the tissue box. It was empty.

Stepan cleared his throat. "When things got difficult for my parents, in Hungary and after, they had to learn how to suffer. How to do things differently."

Lily stared at him. *This isn't about your precious parents*, she wanted to shout. *What do you know, anyway? You had parents. They cared for you, right? Fuck you.* She swiped at her face, furious. "I don't know what you're talking about."

She shifted her gaze to Uncle Herman. "Which hand? Margrit never said, and I forgot to ask."

"The right," he answered. "The cast stays on for six weeks. Then therapy."

"I have to go," Lily repeated.

"You have to eat," he countered. "Hash and eggs. Hope you like it cold."

"You're kidding, right? My grandmother is in the hospital with fucking *pneumonia* and a busted arm, and you want me to *wait*?" Lily shoved her half-eaten dinner away, jumped up, spun around, and grasped the chair's back with both hands.

"Only until school ends," Stepan said. "Two-and-a-half, three weeks. Then go. I'll buy you a plane ticket."

Uncle Herman, washing dishes at the sink, said nothing.

"Well, that's big of you," Lily exploded. "Why is this even your business? It's not your family, so butt out, okay?"

Stepan opened his mouth to reply and closed it again. He jammed his hat on his head and walked out, leaving the back door open behind him. "There's no talking to her," he said through gritted teeth. They heard his car start, the tires grinding on gravel, then silence.

"No shit," Uncle Herman muttered. He turned the water off and reached for a towel. "Guess you don't know a helping hand when you see one."

Lily blanched, then reddened. "And you." She pointed at his back. "Grams is your sister. How much more family you got? You're the one should be driving away. Me, I'd be a hundred miles from here by now."

"Car won't make it," he said. "And it's not your decision." He tossed the towel on the counter. "Nobody tells me what to do or how to feel, least of all a mixed-up kid."

"Oh, sorry," Lily grimaced. "Excuse me for forgetting who the grownups are around here. Man, if I—"

"Enough." Uncle Herman slammed the open door shut. "You finish school, you can do what you want." He slipped past her into the living room and turned on the news.

Lily slumped in her chair. *That went well*, she thought. *The hell happens now?*

30

Gotta go. Can't wait. I've got money for the bus, so I won't be hitchhiking with any creepy strangers. Call you when I get there.

Lily folded the note, then opened it again and added:

Thanks for taking me in, and all.

She placed it, unsigned, on Uncle Herman's bed. At the door she stood a moment, thinking. "Don't be like that," she said. "You know how it feels." She picked up the note, wrote *Lily* across the bottom, and added a quick sketch—a long face with slits for eyes and a shock of unruly hair. "Looks like a goddamn pineapple," she said. She replaced the note on the bed, grabbed her backpack, jammed her money in her jeans pocket, and ran out.

She had sold her almost new winter jacket and boots to a girl in her algebra class. She didn't get as much as she had hoped for—the girl objected to a barely visible stain on the cuffs, some scuffing on the boots, and threatened to walk away from the deal unless the price came down. Lily took the money. Added to the sale of the boom box Stepan had given her, and her stash from Christmas and her birthday, it was enough. It would have to be.

Stepan was waiting in the car, fiddling with the radio dial. After her outburst last week, he'd been distant, but only for a day or two. He wasn't, apparently, one to hold a grudge.

What did she know? These men had known each other for thirty years or more. Who was she to say what characteristics allowed their arrangement to continue, what quirks each valued in the other, or chose to ignore? She had barged in, bringing her own kind of chaos, assuming she could stay because she wanted to, never once considering how her presence might disrupt their lives.

It was the first time he offered to drive her to school since the incident. "You don't have to," she protested, a little shamefaced.

"I know I don't. But I'm done with sales calls until the end of June, so I'll be around, doing paperwork and reading next year's galleys. We've all heard how much you hate riding with the cretins on the school bus. Your words exactly.'

"Well, yeah, okay." She flung her backpack into the back seat.

"What's in there?" Stepan lowered the volume on his morning news program. "What's that rattle?"

"Oh, school project," Lily lied.

"What kind?"

She had to think fast. The night before, she had stuffed her backpack with socks and underwear, a couple of t-shirts, her psychedelic Minnie Mouse pajamas. She sat for a while with the box of her father's postcards open on her lap. She laid them out on the bed, like puzzle pieces or some quirky version of Solitaire. Maybe people who wanted to hide had their reasons. Later, when she was grown, it might make sense. She stacked the cards in reverse order, with the snowman on top, secured them with a rubber band and pushed them into the bottom of the backpack. After a moment, she tossed in a handful of her mother's cassettes. *My inheritance,* she thought.

"Counterculture and politics," she said now to Stepan. "You know, Bobby Kennedy and all. I thought I'd play some music to like, liven things up."

"Sounds interesting." Stepan gave up on the radio, clicked it off.

They rode in silence until Lily burst out, "Listen, I'm sorry I said those things, about you not being family."

"You were right. Forget it."

"No. I mean yes. I was out of my head, with Grams hurt and sick and me so far away. But I had no right."

Stepan looked at her, not smiling but chill, unperturbed. "Forget it."

"Do people ever stop making mistakes? Is that what it means to grow up?"

"No. Growing up is taking the blame, owning up. And fixing it, like you just did."

Lily stared out the window at the now familiar landscape, the cows, farm buildings, newly planted fields. "I'm—" she started to say, then changed her mind. They would know soon enough.

When they reached the strip mall near the school, she said, "Drop me here, please. I'm meeting this kid who helped with my project."

"You sure?"

"Yeah. Thanks." She grabbed her backpack and walked toward the coffee shop, not too fast. She stood outside as if waiting for someone until Stepan's car was out of sight, then headed for the Orange and Green bus depot.

She figured it would be hours before Uncle Herman found the note. Where did he go, anyway? He had no job, or friends she knew about, or obligations. He left the house every morning, came back around noon to fix himself a sandwich. Baloney or cheese, never both at once, with mustard and a garlic pickle. *What an oddball*, she thought. Is that what comes of living alone all those years, with no family to distract him from his routine? All those people dying, one after the other or several at a time. And Nora, the mystery woman who liked to dance. Gone. What did that do to a person? She had never lost anyone, not anyone she'd known, anyone she'd miss. She had not experienced that kind of grief. Maybe lacking that knowledge was the missing piece, the thing that might help her understand her cantankerous great-uncle.

In her life, there was only her mother, a big blank, and her father, a bigger question mark. She still wanted to know why he couldn't come right out and talk to her, why they couldn't know each other like normal people do, as father and child.

And she would, one day. Not now. Now she had to see about Grams.

31

The bus was late. Something about an accident or breakdown in Delaware. They had to send an empty bus down to pick up the passengers and were waiting for its return. Seems a small rural depot had few emergency options.

"So what do I do?" Lily tried to sound calm. The last thing she needed was for some nosy clerk to call in the cops or whatever, making a scene while she tried to explain that no, she wasn't running away, not this time, and losing precious time while they sorted it all out. "My grandmother's expecting me."

The window clerk glanced at the departure schedule—one of those whiteboards with lines for black vinyl letters and numbers to be pressed in by hand as the day progressed. "You could go to Albany. Leaves in thirty-seven minutes. Change there for points west. Or else wait. Shouldn't be more than a couple of hours." He waved a paperback book he was holding toward the entrance door. "There's a pay phone outside."

Points west. She liked the sound of that, the way it made her urgent trip sound like an escapade, an adventure. But she would lose time. And it would cost more, for sure. "I'll wait," she said.

The waiting room was no bigger than an average classroom. Faded photo posters of New York state attractions hung on walls that had once been beige. As if after you've seen Niagara Falls and Rockefeller Center, you might as well stay home. Lily wondered if the molded plastic chair manufacturing industry had a patent on those particular shades of puke green and neon orange—why they seemed to be in use in nearly every bus station she had seen. A dusty speaker under the ceiling leaked lite classical music, tunes she recognized from TV commercials and her seventh-grade music class. "Weird," she said.

A few people with duffle bags or briefcases sat on benches outside. Lily stayed indoors, positioned between the glass entrance door and the emergency exit. She could watch for Stepan or Uncle Herman's car and make her getaway in case they got it into their heads that she needed to be rescued or stopped.

It didn't sound like much of a plan. What would she do once she was out the back door? It was best not to dwell on it. "How much longer?" she asked the clerk.

He tented his book on the counter and rubbed two fingers over his reddish starter mustache. "They departed Newark, Delaware fifty-five minutes ago. Should arrive by eleven twenty-two, conditions permitting."

"You always talk like that? Arrive, depart, conditions permitting?" Lily mimicked.

The clerk took a conductor's cap off its hook and placed it on his head, using both hands to align the visor above his face. He leaned into a stationary microphone. "Passengers for Kingston, Saugerties, Catskill, and Albany may now board at the departures platform. Please secure your belongings and have your ticket ready. Thank you for riding Orange and Green."

He came out of the ticket booth, smoothing the front of his jacket over a nascent beer belly. He threw a dark glance in Lily's direction and strode out to help three elderly men, a woman with two toddlers, a business-suited woman with the *Wall Street Journal* sticking out of her handbag, and a pair of college students in brand-new SUNY sweatshirts onto the waiting bus.

The bus pulled away, leaving a plume of blue exhaust in the

air. Lily thought, *Get me out of here. This place is for the birds. It's California for me from now on. Hang on, Grams. Hang on.*

The waiting room grew warm. A faint odor of diesel fuel wafted through the open door. Lily stared at a cartoon poster showing how to perform the Heimlich maneuver and wondered why a public space this size with two vending machines needed to display it. *Yeah, in case someone chokes on a Cheese Doodle.* She dozed, rousing herself every few minutes to survey the parking lot. Time dragged.

At precisely eleven twenty-two, the bus from Delaware pulled in. Another half-hour passed while it disgorged its weary passengers, fueled up, and had the aisle swept clean of travel debris.

On board at last, Lily dropped her backpack on the window seat right behind the driver and settled in next to it on the aisle. She was in no mood to talk to bored or inquisitive strangers. There were plenty of other seats. Once on the road to Stroudsburg/Scranton/Cleveland/Toledo, she relaxed into the forward motion of the wheels taking her, finally, west.

The driver hummed along to a country music station. Lily could see him tapping his fingers on the steering wheel, then flip a switch under a flashing red button. He squinted up into the rearview mirror. "Yeah, I think so. Right. Got it," he said in response to the incomprehensible crackle of a two-way radio. The bus zoomed along the highway, past budding trees and tall brown grasses, truck stops and industrial warehouses. Lily's glance caught a movement in the driver's side-view mirror: a motorcycle cop, lights flashing, hell-bent on catching some flagrant speeder, was gaining ground in the left lane.

Only there didn't seem to be any speeders; traffic was sparse and orderly. *Maybe that truck up ahead is really a smuggler,* she imagined. *Carrying like, contraband or hiding illegal aliens.*

But no. With the cop nearly alongside, the bus slowed down, turned on its flashers, and pulled onto the shoulder. The cop cut in front of the bus and stopped. Stepan's BMW was right behind him.

"Fuck," Lily said. "Fuck, fuck, fuck."

The bus driver caught her eye in the rearview. "You know him?"

She set her jaw. "Yeah." Whatever happened now, she wasn't going quietly.

She watched Uncle Herman get out of the passenger side of the car. Out of the corner of her eye, she saw Stepan open the trunk and take something out, but her gaze was riveted on the old man, his steps a little shaky, his back straight. He approached the bus. *I'm not going back, not going back, can't make me.*

When the bus door opened and the top of his hat appeared, she said, "Not going..." and stopped, arrested by the look on his face. She saw no anger in it. He looked weary, determined, and maybe, if such a thing were possible in the circumstances, a little bit amused.

"She's old and sick, Uncle Herman. I never should have left her alone, and now she's in the hospital, and I'm a whole country away. What if I don't get there in time?" In the background, Lily heard other passengers moving around, voices questioning the delay, the driver saying, "Okay?" closing the door, putting the bus in gear. She didn't care; she couldn't stop babbling. "My father doesn't care about me, he never did. I'm so stupid, I never should have come. Why didn't you send me back? Old people die from pneumonia every day, what if..."

Uncle Herman slid a ratty gym bag onto the overhead luggage rack. He reached across to the window seat, picked up her backpack and tossed it up there as well. "Shut up," he said. "You forgot this." He dropped the unfinished yellow Christmas scarf, still on its circular knitting needle, in Lily's lap. "Move over."

***

Author's Note

I have heard it said that fiction writers do not invent stories. They discover them. I believe this to be true.

I recently came across a handwritten document that places my grandfather—if his words are to be believed—in a different country when everything I know of family history has him living elsewhere. Is it true? What was he doing there, and why has no one ever talked about it? Here is an intriguing real-life question that mirrors fiction. Everyone who might have answers has died; the secret may never be revealed.

For this writer, the process of composition starts with a character. Who is the story about? What are their attributes, their fears? What do they want, need, lack? So it begins: other characters enter the room, they talk to each other, reveal thoughts and wishes, make demands. Things happen. They learn about each other and about themselves. And we say, yes, that's the way it is. I see now why they behave like that, it couldn't be otherwise. It's who they are.

In this book, Lily and Uncle Herman occupy the main stage. Secondary characters—Stepan and Stella—fill in details, ask questions, keep things moving. The pieces are in place: conflict is revealed; the action is set in motion. We have a story.

And then there's Nora.

Nora doesn't speak or act. She is never in the room. We sense traces of her long-ago presence like a vanished scent, a hint of former occupancy. In her absence, we find no letter or diary or shopping list that may validate her part in the story, yet after thirty-odd years, her spices are still in the kitchen cabinet. For Uncle Herman's near-Spartan lifestyle, this seems like an aberration, a conscious, puzzling decision. The clues we have are enticing but not helpful; Uncle Herman cannot—or will not—explain.

We know Nora was part of his life. We know she walked away. Why, then, are her hats, shoes, dresses, pictures still in Herman's attic? It may have been a temporary arrangement, an amicable favor while she looked for other lodging, or a rift so severe, so wrenching, that coming back for her things was simply impossible. Were there scenes with accusations, recriminations, changed locks? Or maybe nothing at all, the air charged with unspoken words, hearts weighted with regret and broken promises. Like Lily, the reader may wonder, *What's the freakin' mystery?*

Nora is a shadow on Uncle Herman's heart that he guards with near-total silence. When he tells Lily that she liked to dance, he retreats from the intimacy of that revelation into the privacy of his memories, his pain. Nora remains a mystery and, paradoxically, along with the trauma of relentless grief over the loss of his family, the key to his abrasive nature. When he boards the bus with Lily to reconnect with his one remaining sister, we must see the act as momentum, a step, perhaps, toward some measure of healing.

But slowly, now. After all, he packed only a small gym bag for the journey.

And what of Mark, the father Lily barely knows through cryptic postcards, who refuses to come into focus for reasons known only to himself. He admits his fear of the parental role. He sends Stella support money for Lily, but shrinks from taking part in his daughter's life in any meaningful way. But the cards keep coming as if he can't relinquish the connection, all while choosing not to tell where he is, what he's doing, what he thinks or feels. It seems perverse, a maddening game without rules. Who wins, who loses?

The truth is, I don't know. When characters are reclusive, when they choose to shroud their motives in baffling actions, the reticence becomes part of the story.

As for the conundrum of my grandfather's words, that's a mystery to tackle another day.

Acknowledgments

I am grateful to Kevin Atticks of Apprentice House Press for shepherding this book through its developmental stages, and to Jack Barker for editorial assistance. Managing Editor Molly Gerard helped steer the process, Aminah Murray handled promotion details, and Molly Clement contributed design expertise. My thanks to the entire team for their part in bringing an idea, a collection of words, to life, for making it a book.

To Rebecca Fifield's detailed notes addressing areas of clarification and general improvement; it would have been foolish not to take her words to heart.

To the members of the Cornwall Writers Circle for the collegial tough love that kept the vision in focus to the finish, and to Tanya Cramer, for suffering through my spells of doubt with good cheer and eminently useful suggestions.

This book would be a diminished effort without the critical eyes of my manuscript readers—Celia Galorenzo, Jacque Metsma and Jaan Metsma, Robin Schogol and Jonathan Mushlin—whose attentive observations were invariably on point.

Special appreciation to authors Roselee Blooston, Nancy Burke, Alice Elliott Dark, Martin Golan, and A. Molotkov for taking time from their own projects to contribute endorsements. Those generous words mean the world to me.

And, of course, to Frank.

Thank you, all.

About the Author

Marina Antropow Cramer is the child of post-WWII Russian refugees from the Soviet Union. Her work has appeared in Blackbird, Wilderness House, Bloom Literary Magazine, Hobart's NOW, Comstock Review, Pure Slush, and the *other side of hope literary journal*, among other print and online publications. She has served as a workshop instructor at various conferences and festivals. She is the author of the novels *Roads* (Chicago Review Press), *Anna Eva Mimi Adam* (RunAmok Books), and *Marfa's River* (Apprentice House Press), and lives in New York's Hudson Valley.

Apprentice House Press
Loyola University Maryland

Apprentice House is the country's only campus-based, student-staffed book publishing company. Directed by professors and industry professionals, it is a nonprofit activity of the Communication Department at Loyola University Maryland.

Using state-of-the-art technology and an experiential learning model of education, Apprentice House publishes books in untraditional ways. This dual responsibility as publishers and educators creates an unprecedented collaborative environment among faculty and students, while teaching tomorrow's editors, designers, and marketers.

Eclectic and provocative, Apprentice House titles intend to entertain as well as spark dialogue on a variety of topics. Financial contributions to sustain the press's work are welcomed. Contributions are tax deductible to the fullest extent allowed by the IRS.

To learn more about Apprentice House books or to obtain submission guidelines, please visit www.apprenticehouse.com.

Apprentice House Press
Communication Department
Loyola University Maryland
4501 N. Charles Street
Baltimore, MD 21210
Ph: 410-617-5265
info@apprenticehouse.com • www.apprenticehouse.com